# FEATHERS
## TO FILTH

THE ORIGINAL EIGHT

# FEATHERS TO FILTH

## R. J. JEFFREY

First published in Great Britain in 2012 by
FeedARead

This edition published in Great Britain in 2012 by
FeedARead

Thank you to all my family who have encouraged to
me write this book.

Special thanks to my Grandmother and Sister for
taking the time to read this and give feedback.

Also, thank you to you for choosing to read this first
book of the Feathers to Filth series.

# Heavens
# Law

- - - - - - - - - - -

No God shall interfere with Mortal affairs

No God shall harm a being of the Mortal realm

No God shall abandon their duty

No God shall engage in the creation of another

If any break the laws that are given,
the choice of punishment shall fall to the First

# Chapter I

-

# The Prisoner

"It's cold, Hermes." whimpered a shaking voice in the darkness. "Why is it so cold?"

The old stone walls echoed with the distant beating of spear against shield.

"What a ridiculous question." snapped Hermes with a bitter tone. "You honestly believed that your sins would go unpunished."

The beat of steel was accompanied by a unified roar of men.

"A sin is a matter of perspective, granted, it is regrettable that any man woman or child should lose their lives in this unholy conflict. Although, I recognize that there was nothing that could be done for the thousands that were sucked below sea." replied the dusty, weak voice.

"Perhaps if you had actually attempted to protect the island's shores you wouldn't be here."

"Are you implying that I abandoned them?!" screamed the man, his rage underlined by the screech and grinding of chains against rock. "I suffered within an inch of my life to save them! You know this! You witnessed it for yourself."

A short pause flooded the cell, before hollow footsteps bounded its length. Suddenly, the room was alit with a dim, sunburst glow. Hermes, engulfed in the light, stood before the shackled man. His gleaming, golden hair flowed around his slim, toned shoulders, as if joined in a dance with his shimmering drapes, which were strapped at his waist with a bold leather strap.

He crouched down to the man's level, resting his forearms upon his own knees.

"I told you that you have sinned, do not frustrate your regret by confronting me here. You know that your crimes in this world go hand in hand with those you committed as a God."

The shackled man raised his head, his face glistening as beads of sweat trickled from his creased brow, running along his chiselled jaw and dripping from his stubble coated chin. His and Hermes shining yellow eyes locked, the man's oily black locks also began to waft. The pair stared in temper.

Although, it was abruptly broken by the prolonged howl of a massing army, heading to war. The man's attention quickly darted towards a small, barred window on the far wall.

"Hermes, why don't they allow me to battle alongside them? They know my abilities can at the least even the odds."

Hermes straightened his posture and turned away.

"Please! Free me! If you don't, more and more of them will march to their death! By leaving me contained in here, you, will be responsible for this."

Hermes quickly swung around, his cape giving a delayed whip. "I was the being who forged those chains and aided the King of this land in keeping you imprisoned here!" His voice thundered with almighty presence.

The man's eyes widened as his chamber burst into light, yellow steams prancing around in furious elegance. His large, muscular figure trembled tamely, never before being present during one of Hermes's outbursts.

"And as such, I am unable to break those chains that bind you." He began to back away, his aura fading. "You have fallen from the realm above, in this land you are considered a monster!" Hermes paused slightly as his gaze shifted to the ground, his expression sinking. "I am sure I need not remind you of the world that awaits you should you falter once more."

The prisoner gasped in realization. "No! Hermes you can't leave me here! I may be mortal now but I was once your brother, an Original God! If I am to be trapped in this polluted realm then at very least allow me to be present with my former greatness!" He pleaded. "Restore the power that I once possessed and-"

"Farewell…" Hermes began.

"You spineless bastard! May the Devil take pity on your blackened soul! A Throne of bones awaits you by his side!"

"…And may the First bless you, brother Wrath." He concluded, his eyes filling up.

In a dense white flash, he vanished. A single tear fell and burst against the stone, drowning out the noise of the army, whom were destined to die.

Wrath felt his throat tighten, a cannonball of sorrow pulling in his chest. "Please….don't leave me in this place. I…I can't…I don't…." His sentence remained unfinished as he began to weep. He rocked from his knees and crashed to his side, curling his body as he felt the chains tighten.

# Chapter II

-

# An Impossible Enemy Part 1

"Today, we face our enemy! Not to defeat him! Not to bring him to his knees! But to slaughter him where he stands! And turn this battlefield into a bloody grave!" Encouraged the Commander of the Fifth Legion. "Even one thousand years from now, this spot will be known for our victory!"

The army, ten thousand strong, thumped their shields in response, fuelled by their leaders' words and their own sheer adrenaline.

"This is the hour the Prophets have predicted, that the enemy will once again show his damned face in our land!"

The shields were beaten three times.

"And when he does, who shall he face?!"

"Herateas! Herateas!" The army chanted.

"And we will be sure to make it a name to remember." The Commander spoke proudly, turning to face over the cliff at the calm crystal sea, as it caressed the rocky face. The sky was painted a misty blue, a narrow blanket of cloud rolled softly by. Ten thousand warriors panted heavily in anticipation, eager to commence in their battle, the battle that would surely engrave their names in legend. But they must wait, wait until the enemy decides to once again visit their land.

They stood, heavy with armour blessed by the Prophets, shields and spears clasped tight, swords hanging from the hip as a comforting friend. A mass of shining steel, broken by a hundred rippling, red banners, pointing from the sea.

Hours past, shoulders began to droop, knees trembled with exhaustion. Regardless, the Commander stood tall before his men, shoulders back, knees locked, chest out, his hands resting patiently on the hilt of his blade. His mind and vision immersed in the sight of the warm orange sun as it touched the horizon, ever aware that his foe could appear without warning, ever aware that any moment could be his last.

Finally, the sun gave its last ray of the day, plunging out of sight. The soldiers had endured hours of blistering heat, and were finally gifted with the cool kiss of night. However night also brought its own infectious fear. The enemy could see in the dark, man could not. The enemy thrived in shadowed battle, man was hindered. For some, it would be their first act of War. These few individuals were still empowered by passion and desire to bring the adversary to its bloody knees. The experienced among them however, were gradually overcome with memories of previous attempts at victory, and how brutally outmatched they were. Men began to quietly sob, others vowed revenge and once again prepared themselves. The aggressive troops randomly bashed their shields against their body, shaking their head, bouncing on their toes in an attempt to focus and restore some courage.

It was quickly made apparent, that no combat would commence that night. Tents were erected, fires were lit. For the first time since they left home, the men gorged themselves on rare, succulent meat, juicy fruits and fluffy bread. The night of worry was soon transformed into a joyful intoxicated gathering. Soldiers laughed and drank and quickly forgot their reason for being there, losing themselves in ecstasy.

Hidden inside the Commanders tent however, the atmosphere was very different. He sat at the head of a grand oak table, surrounded by his finest Captains, anxiously twirling his goblet on the surface, deep in thought.

"Commander, permission to speak freely?" Questioned a young captain nervously, climbing to his feet.

The Commanders head slightly rose from his palm as he glanced towards his comrade. "Go ahead Vixrol, it saves us sitting here in silence at least." He granted before sinking back onto his palm.

"Well sir, if I may be so bold, perhaps the Prophets misread the future this time? Maybe there is to be no conflict." Vixrol continued.

"Don't be so blind Vixrol!" Argued another captain opposite, oil for the lamb leg he was chewing, dripped and splashed from his ageing, messy beard. "The Prophets have not been mistaken yet and if it weren't for them, Herateas would have burnt to the ground generations ago." He finished, taking another mouthful of meat.

"Well if this is true, where is the enemy?" Vixrol shrugged, looking the length of the table, hoping for a logical response. "Is the possibility of an error not what preys upon your mind, my Commander?" He turned his attention to the head.

The Commander stared blindly to his side, chewing a grape. "No." He concluded. Vixrols' posture fell in disappointment. "The Prophets prediction is not what troubles me." He informed, rising from his bench.

"Well then may I ask what you are pondering?" Vixrols' soft silky voice grew tense and sharp.

"I have a better idea, how about I ask you all, my twelve finest men, a little golden question." This in itself was not a question.

The captains looked at each other, unsettled by their lack of such a 'golden question'.

"Please Brekos, continue." allowed the most elderly captain, clearly comfortable with the Commander due to his manner of address.

Brekos began to stride around the tent. "Thank you Gorton."
Gorton nodded once with appreciation.

"Alright, now this will take some time to process but please, make no rush. I can't seem to solve the answer myself so perhaps one of you can help me?" He appealed, opening his arm to address his company. "Why, now do not jump to conclusions." His expression stiffened as he filled with seriousness and pure frustration. "Why are we not yet dead men?"

The air felt thick as the world fell silent. The captains did not fail to sense Brekos true question.

"You think the enemy is already here?" Vixrol answered, leaning forward and resting his fingertips against the oak.

"I do not think this, Vixrol, I know it."

"But then why have they not attacked?" Gorton said, sieving through the riddles.

"You and I have faced this kind of foe many time Gorton and every time they have swiftly and easily broken through our ranks." His head tilted back a little. "They do not hide, because they do not fear us. They do not wait for nightfall, because they do not need the advantage."

"So?" Gorton insisted, shaking his head and shuffling in his place, his thick beaded hair swaying at his chest.

"They are waiting for something. Not an advantage. Not a command since they do not compose themselves for battle…they want something, quietly."

"Well invite them for a drink, show some hospitality!" Vixrol gestured mockingly.

"Watch your tongue boy." Brekos snapped.

"No sir I will not! Your suggestion is ridiculous and has only succeeded in dampening our last hours of peace! You're growing old and confused Commander, perhaps…" Vixrol took a deep breath and hesitated.

"Say it boy…" Brekos summoned. Vixrol did not respond. "Say it!" he boomed.

"Perhaps it is time you enrolled a new Commander…"

The hall was silent once more, all apart from the crackling of the torches which were spaced around the edge. Brekos paced calmly towards Vixrol, stopping within striking distance. Vixrol stepped from his stool to meet his superior.

"F-f-f-forgive me Commander." He stuttered, avoiding eye contact. "It's been a long tense day that I would rather it be done with."

"I understand that you are anxious to lead these men and reach your potential. I believe you could do so, after all the Prophets proclaimed you as the Prodigy Child. A man who could change the world just by existing." Brekos praised.

"Thank you sir." He bowed.

"And one day you will be Commander."

Vixrol smiled, finding the comfort to make eye contact.

"But you will not lead this army."

His eyes narrowed, puzzled as he took a small step forward. He smiled once again. "Brekos I thi-"

Suddenly, Brekos lifted his athletic right leg, and pounded it into Vixrols' stomach, hard enough to split his leather bound sandal, launching him towards the doorway. He bounced before squirming in agony, unable to breathe.

"I, Commander Brekos Eastartes of the Fifth Legion, hereby strip you of your rank and rule!"

Gorton shakily sprung to his feet. "Brekos please! Have some mercy he's just a lad!"

"I furthermore banish you from serving our King in war or in peace!"

Vixrol struggled to roll to his knees, propping himself on an elbow, gasping for breath, blood trickling from his moist lips, staining the rug below.

"Now get out of my sight, and should I ever see you again, I will cut that cursed tongue from your head." He panted in anger, looking down at his outcast.

Vixrol turned his head back, his dark weaved plats dangling at his cheek. His eyes pink and dripping with upset and pain. The captains stood in their seats, looking down at him in disgust, all apart from Gorton, who could not turn his gaze from Brekos. He however, was shaking with fury.

The breathless Vixrol clambered towards the exit, stumbling out of sight, his hand clutching his stomach.

The patter of horse hoof against dry mud could be heard, getting dimmer, followed by a drunken chant.

Meanwhile, back in the tent, Gorton spoke out. "We are about to head into a whole hell of shit and you just exiled one of our best warriors, not to mention the sharpest mind in all ten thousand men!"

Brekos remained speechless, as did the others. His gasps had calmed to a steady, open mouthed pant.

"Can you not even see reason past your pride man? Or do you envy his title?"

Again, not so much as an utter.

"Speak man!" Gorton begged.

Just as he had finished his cry, he noticed that the Commanders breathing had slowed completely. He was still, not so much as a twitch or flinch. He was stiff, until he steadily dropped to his knees. The captains briskly dived to his aid, catching him by the shoulder, lowering him to the ground and straightening out his legs.

"What happened?" Queried a Captain.

"He's not breathing!" Informed another.

"What in the hell is going on?!" Gorton cried.

"My my, this certainly is a most concerning event." Declared a soothing, sexy voice.

The soldiers jumped in shock as they were confronted by an elegant, young woman, perched on the edge of the table, examining a deep red apple. A dark silk dress dangled from her tiny shoulders, flipping and folding, exposing her impressive cleavage. It waved down her body, cutting off at her gracefully flawless thighs, one hooked over the other.

"Who are you, whore? How long have you been present?" Questioned a captain as he drew his sword, oil still spilling from his beard.

The women burst into laughter. "Whore?" she giggled again. "Oh come now, I have no fault in my mind that men such as yourselves have often longed for a 'whore' such as myself to be presented to you." She teased, tracing the neat polished nail of her middle finger up her shin, over her knee, and finally halting as she slightly edged up the base of her dress. "Wouldn't you agree?"

"Do not interpret my gaze as lust, fiend." defended the bearded man.

"Hold your insults mortal!" Instructed the new arrival, her voice, though sweet, was surrounded by a demonic echo.

The torches lashed and quietly fizzled out. In any other situation the world would be in shadow. Though due to hundreds of campfires and the thin cloths used for the shelter, they were blessed with a dull gift of vision.

Gorton froze in horror. Lining the red and white striped sheet, were the shadows of dozens of men, hanging in the air, like the silhouettes of a criminals at the gallows, with no evidence of a rope or frame.

"What sorcery is this?" Gorton mumbled, stepping back.

The woman skipped from the desk, her luscious shimmering curls jiggled as she landed. "I know not what you refer to, human?" She paraded towards Gorton, her toes barely skimming the ground. "Do you refer to the meaningless casts that float before you?" she brushed the back of her fingers along Gortons' wrinkled jaw. "Or do you refer to the spark we feel when our lives entwine?" She whispered submissively.

She lazily closed her eyes, her lips apart. She became weightless as she pulled herself up by the back of Gortons' neck, slowly and steadily. Once she was at his eye level, she leant forwards, pressing her plump inviting lips gently against his.

He felt an odd tingling sensation cover his body. It was familiar to him. Like the first time he had kissed his late wife when he was a young man in his prime. Every trace of fear and rage drained from his being. He felt new again. His lips perked willingly, surrendering to his desires. Then, his skin felt tight, however his body felt stronger. He winced in aggravation, only to then find himself more entranced by this strange woman. As soon as he had totally lost connection to the real world, the woman broke the kiss, closing it with a soft, flirtatious nibble of his bottom lip as she pulled away. Gorton opened his eyes once more, his skin still feeling tight. The other captains stood in awe.

"Well Captain Gorton, I bet you have broken a heart or two in your time with a face like that." She complimented, coated with surprise.

"Forgive me my lady." He chuckled. "But I am well past my time of pleasure."

"Oh I would deeply disagree."

Gorton turned his attention to a mirror-like golden tray, settled on the table, a bounty of fruit upon it. With one last glance at the woman, he hastily hurried over to it, grabbing it and spilling the fruit across the table. He positioned it in front of his 'heart breaking face', firmly holding it at both sides. It was too dark to see any reflection. Then he noticed his hands. They were someone else's. No, they were his but… different. Without warning, the torches once again burst into life, blinding him for a brief moment. As his vision returned, he saw himself. Though it was not as he recalled, he was slimmer, bolder. He dropped the plate in disbelief and backed into a thick wooden trunk, the support beam for the tent. "I…I am…" He threw his head back, shifting his eyes towards the woman. "I am young again." He wept, tears tumbling down his hairless cheeks.

The woman swayed with self-gratification, linking her hands behind her back.

"I'm glad you like it my darling, but now I wish for something in return."

"Which is?" He pondered.

"Will you come with me?" she tilted her head in a cute fashion. "Come and rule by my side and be mine for eternity?"

Gortons' mood snapped right back to how it was, furious and full of blood lust. "Absolutely not you devil! I may have fallen for your appeal but I will never desert my duty!"

"Oh?" she moved a hand and placed it on her hip. "Well then I suppose you can't own me anymore."

The woman abruptly pranced towards the other bearded captain, and stood up on a single set of toes, bending her other leg, again, closing her eyes and leaning in for a kiss.

"NO!" Gorton howled passionately, pulling a dagger from his belt and flinging it with new found strength into the captains' ribs. Though it did not stop, it penetrated his entire body, leaving a hollow crater through him. Blood spewed out of his wound, cascading down his armour into a puddle. He looked down, unable to feel. With his last ounce of life he looked to Gorton with cold, empty eyes. The woman nudged his arm, sending him tumbling down, landing in his puddle, spraying it onto the woman's feet.

"Such a messy creature." she said as she kicked his head, barefoot, smashing his skull. It would be the first glimpse of her cruel nature.

Gorton glanced down at his hand, shaking with fear and yet he felt like a King. Was this woman really capable of giving him such gifts?

"Darling?" addressed the woman. "Are you coming?" she began to make her way out of the tent.

He looked up at her, indecisive, his eyes jolting from left to right, unable to come to an answer.

"Darling…" she said firmly.

# Chapter III

-

# Chosen Grief

After hours of riding, with no real haste, a rock and iron metropolis climbed over the horizon, a welcome contrast to the murky meadow. The mousy brown steed ferried Vixrol to the gates of the city, only to be confronted by four heavily armed guards.

"Sir, forgive my obstruction." Began one of the guards, the only one among them not hidden by a helmet. "It is unlike you to ride unattended, especially given your position."

Vixrol kept his head down, shrouded by a thick red hooded cloak, his hands loosely holding the reins.

"Sir, I'm afraid I must insist you provide evidence that you are in fact Captain Vixrol, and not some damned impostor." The guard insisted, revealing an inch of his silver blade as he pulled it from its sheath out of caution. The other guards soon did the same.

Vixrol glanced through a small opening in his hood, up at the city wall. It was decorated with at least twenty archers, all prepared to fire. Unfortunately for Vixrol, he knew that the archers were famous for their killing blows.

Reluctantly, he hopped off his horse, squelching into a muddy puddle, ankle deep.

The guard drew another inch. "Sir I must insist."

The captain presented his right arm to the soldier, his palm to the sky as he clenched his fist. The guards focus shifted from the arm to Vixrol, then, he swiftly drew his sword, using the tip of it to shuffle the sleeve of the damp, crimson drapes. His method soon revealed a strange symbol, etched into his arm, resembling some form of star.

The inspector smiled politely, lowering his weapon. "Thank you Sir, though out of curiosity, why do you ride alone?"

Vixrol leaped back onto his panting horse, trotting inside the city without gracing the man with an answer.

The splatter of muddy hooves gradually shifted into an empty knocking as he travelled through the cobble streets. Passing market stalls and homeless, battered children, he finally reached the entrance to his quarters. He slumped from his mustang, struggling to find the will to stand, though somehow, he managed. Dragging himself to the stairs, he began to climb the spiralling case. He was hidden from sight by a thick, secure tower, surrounding the ascent. His body felt heavy, his arms hanging by his side, his legs slowly crumbling beneath him. The pita-pata of his feet against the stairway clapped in the echo.

"Sire? Is that you?" Peeped a gentle voice.

Suddenly an elegant, slender woman emerged from a small archway, several stairs ahead of Vixrol. She turned, her hair tied up in a messy bunch on top of her head, and smiled innocently as she saw her 'sire', just as he folded his hood to the back of his neck.

"My lord it is so good to meet you again." she bowed, resting her hands on her stained apron.

"You may drop this irritating act Gabriella. I come alone." Vixrol uttered, his first words since his outburst back on the battlefield.

Gabriellas' face sank, although inside she was thrilled they were alone.
"Darling what happened? Is it not a gift that you return alive?" She placed a hand on his cheek as he approached. "You are not usually this grim after a battle. Did you lose many men?"

Vixrol slapped her arm away and walked into the room she came from. She followed.

"Vixrol you cannot hold yourself responsible for the death of your men. War is a creation that devours souls." She continued, resting her hands on his shoulders, squeezing slightly. "You are a great captain Vixrol and an even better man, no one can question that."

"I am no captain." he whispered, his head in his hand, his shoulders tense as his 'maid' gripped them from behind.

"I'm sorry darling, I couldn't hear wh-"

"I am no captain!" He bellowed, spinning on the spot, flinging her arms away, knocking her off balance. "And for that matter I am barely even an excuse for a man."

He tweaked the link on his collar, loosening his cape and letting it fall to the floor around him.

"Why do you say such things?" Gabriella asked, a lump in her throat.

"I say these things because they are true. I confronted my Commanders honour." He ripped a band of armour from his bicep and tossed it across the room. "I was stripped…" He unfasten the straps on another. "…of my rank!" Again, he tore it from his body and threw it against the sandy plastered wall.
Gabriella covered her mouth in fear and shock, her eyes began to glisten as she backed up against the thick wooden door, closing it.

Vixrol leant with his fists pressed hard against another oak desk. "But worst of all…" He gave it a gentle thump. "Worst of all I know that without me they will all die!" He repeatedly punched the desk, caving its surface, so hard that it began to splinter. Each time he withdrew his arm, speckles of blood leapt from his knuckles.

Gabriellas' face morphed from horror to confusion. "Vixrol?" She started. He continued to pound his frustration into the desk. "Vixrol!"

"What!" He cried, panting, wincing in pain from his shattered hands.

"You mean to say that there was no battle?"

"This is exactly what I am telling you. The Prophets were wrong." He cradled his hands, examining the damage.

"Are you doubting our sacred guardians? The very people who gave you an immense honour, simply as a birth right?"

"I do not doubt their judgement however their ability to foresee must be fading. In addition to this, the Commander had the arrogance to suggest that the enemy was actually waiting. Waiting, can you believe that? Creatures who do not stop until they are dead, were waiting, wanting something without striking a blow."

The atmosphere suddenly took a sinister switch.

"Although…his army is now out there, also waiting, nowhere near the city. At least a days march. That is providing they are actually alive."

"Vixrol where does this talk come from? This is not like you. You are not the man who stole my heart."

"And you were but a starving slut!" Vixrols' words seemed to pierce a hole through her. Her lips twitched as her eyes squinted.

"Is that still how you envision me? As a common street mite?" She narrowly whimpered.

"The King is defenceless with his finest out of the city." He stated, overlooking the question. "And I so happen to have the one man who he fears most."

Quickly, Gabriellas' need for an answer vanished. "Vixrol! You wouldn't! Why would you even think that?!"

Vixrol grinned madly. "And that man just so happens to be a vessel of anger, dying for revenge."

Gabriella was stunned once again, horrified at what her beloved was suggesting. Without another word, Vixrol, drunk with potential, shoved his maid to the floor, her head closely missing the solid metal bed frame. He creaked the door open, slamming it behind him, dust exploding from the hinges. He sprinted down the stairs with thundering steps, the bawling weeps from the room quickly dying out. Rain burst against his grubby skin as he darted across the courtyard, hustling through a crowd of working civilians. Baskets and barrels littered the ground as he forced his path, several of them splitting open, oozing with rare red wine.

Soon, he was sheltered by a grand, derelict chapel. Pristine, divine paintings decorated the ceiling, disrupted by thick, weaving ivy. Huge marble pillars stood tall, burdening the weight of its immense load.

Vixrols' eyes rolled up towards the artwork. It reminded him of his childhood. The idea of Angels and Gods, delivering gifts to the Earth. Gifts of food and water, children and shelter. Now though, as a man, the undoubtable truth was this. No matter how badly mankind needed their assistance, no matter how they prayed and pleaded, the Gods would never intervene with the cycle of the world.

Across the way resided a shadowed narrow doorway, hidden by denser undergrowth. He took a deep breath and raised his chest, boldly making his way across the tiled platform, entering the hallway. Eerily, he paused, unsettled by an instinct which he could not describe. He felt threatened and vulnerable, as though he was entering a sealed cage with a tortured, enraged animal. Every fibre of his body was trying to turn away, but he pressed on, driven by his resolve to take his rightful place as ruler of Herateas. His persistence was not rewarded well, very soon he was blocked by a dead end, a solid barrier of stone and mortar.

He sighed with frustration, tapping his forehead against his barricade. It was wet. He silently smirked with delight. The rain could not have reached the wall, it was simple too well cloaked by the chapel. This meant that the wall was newly constructed and easily breachable. This all confirmed that the rumours of his new 'friend's' location were correct. But how could one man demolish an entire wall, which no doubt was built with thick, strong rock. Why else would it be there otherwise.

He pondered for a short while, examining his surroundings for some form of assistance. A chisel, a mallet maybe, but nothing leapt out at him. He wondered outside again, listening to the choir of drizzling pings. A harsh breeze tumbled through the structure, crawling up his spine. He shivered. Then, it came to him. Water expands when it freezes. If there was enough moisture in that wall, he could smash it apart by freezing it. He cautiously scanned the area for signs of any prying eyes. There were none to be seen.

He slithered back towards the obstruction, placing a hand firmly upon it, pushing slightly, his elbow level with his shoulder. The wall began to chill his hand as his eyes closed and his breathing became steady yet deep. Small icy crystals began to spread across the brick, like the ivy on the outside. It grew and grew until it covered its entire face, like a network of twinkling veins. He took one last deep breath.

"Ricktos unro, elcatimai shatrul lec frozdeearin." he chanted quietly. "Trithom sunt terados!"

The frozen complex thickened, jabbing at the wall with tiny, furious pricks, lowering the temperature through and through. In virtually no time at all, his hindrance was now a mass of creaking, groaning ice. Removing his hand, he withdrew a couple of paces, backing away to a safe distance. With a ferocious pop, the wall exploded in all directions, boulders and grit blistered through the air. Vixrol was showered in dirt as he shielded his eyes. As the tumbling crash vanished, he glanced up over his arms. His plan was a success. Before him was a wide, dripping entrance, a clear path into the chamber he had been seeking.

He pranced over the rubble, supporting himself on the jagged stone that remained, keen yet careful not to injure himself.

"You realise that the use of magic outside of a ceremony is an affront to the Gods as well as a brutal abuse of mans' law?" warned a deep voice of authority.

Vixrol looked up, clambering through the passage. There, before him, stood a man in the centre of the room, long dark hair veiling his face. He looked weak, despite the fact his body was hard, each muscle alive and ready for any physical task. He was a statue, tall and solid, facing his guest. There was no doubt in Vixrols' mind that this was the man who would become a crucial part of his plan.

"You, you must the Wrath." he assumed, crouching to a knee, bowing his hand and placing his fist over his heart. "It is a true honour to be in your presence."

"Do not smother me with compliments and false respect. I know why you come here, former Captain Vixrol." Wrath contradicted.

Vixrol threw his head back, just enough to glance through the layers of oily hair, revealing a yellow glowing iris. He felt his body tremble. How is it that a prisoner, who had never been introduced, not only knew his name, but also knew things that only those present during his exile, and Gabriella knew.

"Make no mistake, my respect is not false. Though any compliment I may have given, was by all means a misunderstanding." Vixrol smiled with pride as he began to stand, striding towards the shackled man. "I respect you for your ability to take a life with no remorse, for your will to rip worlds apart to reach your objective. But you are nothing here."

27

Wrath flinched, struggling to control his temper, his arms tensing as the chains cut into his flesh.

"In our land, you are a criminal. Nothing but a man who is merely here because we have yet to find a solution to ending you." Vixrol taunted.

"Be careful human, one day you will have your, what was it…" he paused in thought. "Cursed tongue cut from your head, I believe it was."

The former captain was locked in a speechless fear. It seems that this man knew, word for word, the last thing that the Commander spoke. It wasn't possible. Wrath had been imprisoned for just shy of a year. He could he know.

"What's wrong, boy? Have you exhausted your authority already?" Wrath slowly approached his guest, with eyes alit with heavenly light, he gazed down at him. "Do not speak to me as though we are different. We are the same, to a point. Our means and crimes may never touch, but like it or not, we are both 'criminals' in this land. Exiles from the Kings services and military."

Being in the presence of a God of any sort was a mammoth emotional experience, and it was starting to take its toll. Vixrols' eyes began to burn, desperate to water. It was soon followed by a heavy block in his neck. He knew he was beginning to lose control of his nerves.

"Do not compare me to a sinner like you!" he bellowed in an attempt to distract himself. "I am the Prodigy Child! Hand chosen by the Proph-"

"By the Prophets of Hereteas without whom, everyone would have perished long ago." Wrath interjected, plunging Vixrol into yet another silence.

A tear rolled down his cheek. "How do you know the truths you speak?" he wept.

"Must I remind you that I was not always a man, starved of freedom. I used to be a God." He answered, whipping his hair from his face as he turned, his guest still unable to identify him. "You are endlessly surprised at my knowledge, even of events which I have not witnessed with my own eyes. Perhaps if I explain in greater depth, you will understand." He turned once more, to face Vixrol. As he lay his eyes on Wraths true face for the first time, he was overwhelmed. Tears began to stream down his cheeks, taking with them some dirt from his face.

"I am Wrath, one of the Original Eight. Eight divine beings, created with the single purpose of ensuring the functionality of this realm. Each of us were permitted with certain duties. At first, mine was to ensure that the stars in the entire cosmos burned and raged bright enough to sustain life on various planets." he began.

"I do not understand this talk. You mean to say that those rocks in the Vast Empty have beings like us?"

"One day you will learn." He continued. "However, as I am sure you have discovered through years of whispers,

29

I was exiled from my home realm for my sins, and sent here to protect mankind from our fallen brothers."

Vixrol slumped to the floor, his hands clamped like vice onto the sides of his head. "You do not make sense. You're insane." he murmured.

"As I told you before there were eight of us." Wrath began to lose his composed manner. "What do you think happens when one of us breaks our holy law?"

Vixrol looked up with blank confusion, his lips quivering as tears continued to flow.

"At first, we were sent to what you refer to as Hell, the Underworld. All those sent there become twisted in their own anger and pity, until they are no longer themselves. As more of us fell, our law was changed. The level of tasks per God became too great and as such we were punishable by other means. I am the first to be judged by this new law."

Vixrols' eyes squinted as Wraths glowed with recollection of power.

"As opposed to being sentenced to damnation, I was sent here, as I explained earlier. Although if I fail my duties, I will too fall below this world. In other words, this is my purgatory."

Once again, Vixrol hung his head and shielded it with his hands. "And what if people from this world fail, and sin as a response?" he queried.

"Then you shall fall into Hell and have the displeasure of meeting my brother." Cautioned the fallen God.

Vixrol tensed into a ball, blubbering like a terrified child. He rocked to his side and flopped to the ground. "Then I am as good as damned."

"No Vixrol, you are not."

He stopped crying briefly, looking to Wrath for proof of his contradiction.

"You came here with every intention of forging a pact with me. I would give you your kingdom and in return, you would return my freedom. Just look at you. Nothing but a coward!"

"I do not force these tears, nor can I explain my fear."

"No. You are not a coward for fearing me. I give you that title because you are here at all. You were not foreseen as the Prodigy Child by chance, the Gods do cherish your existence, although your purpose has not relayed its way to me. Go back to your ranks, ride as hard as you can and stand by your Commanders side once again."

"He will never accept me now, I am banished." He recalled, shuffling up onto his arm.

"If you take my words as truth, then heed what I am to tell you." Wrath said, looking directly into Vixrols' puddles of eyes. "My brother will not be as forgiving to mankind as I am."

Vixrol gasped in shock, springing to his feet and wrapping a hand around a chain, looping from Wraths neck, pulling it tight towards him. "You mean to tell me that they will lose if I am not there?!"

"You idiot!" Wrath leant over, locking eyes with his guest. "I am telling you they have already lost."

Vixrols' breaths became shaky and unsteady with realisation of his error. He released his hold on Wrath and backed away, to the hole he created.

"Now, will you fight as a warrior, or let them die without their finest captain among them?"

Vixrol didn't hesitate, he dove through the tunnel, sprinting back to the city. He wiped his face, smearing his tears.

"Excellent decision, Commander Vixrol…"

# Chapter IV

-

# An Impossible Enemy Part 2

"Commander! Commander I beg of you, please wake up!" Pleaded a panicking, inexperienced soldier. "They're going to end us sir! End us!" He grabbed Brekos by the shoulders, shaking him desperately. The Commander was still totally motionless, no signs of life at all. The soldiers' attention darted between his superior and the exit of the blazing tent. He cried out, in undecided frustration, before quickly dropping Brekos back to the ground, fleeing the trap. As he emerged from the fiery structure, a stabbing sense of agony spread throughout his body. He tried to ignore it and run back into the battle, yet he was paralysed. A cold, oily liquid filled his mouth, dribbling from his lips and down to this chest. He glanced, only to see the cause of his pain.

A hand, dripping with his blood, tore through his chest. His heart was resting gently in its grip, pumping slowly, only getting slower. A twisted chuckle voiced behind him. Turning his head he saw an unfamiliar face.

"You....you are the enemy?" He spluttered.

"No my boy." The voice replied, its face dancing and flickering due to passing embers. It leant forward, inches from the dying mans' eyes. "You are the enemy now." With one firm clutch, the soldiers' heart split like a rotten apple, its juice streaming outward. He fell to the ground, his arteries stretching and tearing loose. His heartless corpse topped the bloody, stained earth. It was soon accompanied by his squashed heart, which the murderer tossed to his feet. A bright boom from a nearby campfire lit up the victors' wicked expression of delight.

"You seem to enjoy dismembering them like that, my darling Gorton." The sorceress praised.

"The heart is the centre and creator of love and compassion, these traits will never be permitted amongst vermin in our kingdom, my precious Queen Lilith." Gorton smiled to his new bride of evil.

"I couldn't agree more." She lovingly wrapped herself around his arm.

They both gazed joyfully at the destruction that was unfolding. A battle between man and demon, waged across the cliffs. The blazing flames highlighted every swing and slice, while explosions of gushing blood showered the sky.

"Come, I have something I wish you to see." Lilith tugged gently. Gorton wilfully followed, unable to deny her wishes. She escorted him over to a mound of human carcases. The bodies were still seeping, their faces so scarred that they no longer had an identity. "One day, one day soon, all men shall look like this."

Gortons' lips pulled, resisting a smile. "No." he cried, shaking his head as he freed his arm. "This is no future, let alone a future that I would choose." He diverted his eyes, unable to look at his bride or the small hill of death. His fist crunched, reminding him that he himself had taken several lives with his bare hands as a test of his new strength.

"Gorton when I pressed my lips against you, do you seriously think that I was blind to your desires?"

He responded with a simple flick of his eyes.

"I saw, what you want most." She teased, scraping her nails across his neck and shoulders as she circled him. "You wish for power, and an army, and to be everything that the king is and more. Think, you could be Gorton, King of the Underrealm."

Her words leaked into Gortons' mind, caressing his soul with temptation. He closed his eyes in an act of rational thought.

"Yes, you know me well, yet if I were to accept your proposition, I would be opposition to a new level of foe."

"Hmm…You must expand on this 'new level of foe'?"

"I speak of course of Wrath." He kept his eyes sealed.

"Wrath? Wrath!? That lowly weakling? He is who you fear? He is but a man now, powerless. You can rip men apart with ease and he is still of your concern?" Lilith protested.

Gorton opened his eyes and looked down at her, tucked behind his shoulder. "We have tried all manner of torture and execution to kill him, none of them are effective. He cannot be slain."

She smiled with twisted realisation of yet another opportunity to pull his strings. "You are right, he cannot be killed." She heightened to her tip toes and whispered in his ear. "Not by man at least…"

Gorton felt alive with limitless capability. It surged through his veins with the simple thought that he was able to kill a God. His posture altered from a slump of uncertainty to a tower of pride.

"My dear…" He addressed.

"Yes my King?" She replied.

"Bring him to me." Once again a smile of bloodlust polluted his handsome face.

Lilith chuckled innocently into her lovers' chest, retreating from her toes. "There is no need for me to act upon your request."

Gorton turned his head to her, disappointed and puzzled.

"He comes to us, all I can confirm is that he is close." She concluded, flicking her fingers through her hair.

"Impossible. He cannot break free of those chains. They were forged by Hermes and the King himself."

"Hmm…Sorry darling, but I believe that you are king here." Lilith hushed with her silver tongue.

"You know of what I speak." Frustration and need for a concrete answer filled his voice.

"Lay your fear to rest Gorton, he is still imprisoned. For now at least."

"You told me that he approached." Gorton boomed.

"Oh please, he used to be a God, you honestly think that chains can totally restrict his will?" She questioned as she turned away, walking several paces.

Suddenly there was a spine tingling screech from the battlefield. The King and Queen quickly darted their heads, searching for its origin. The human army had become more organised, bolder, braver. They swarmed around each enemy in small squads, five to ten strong.

"What is this?!" Lilith barked at the sight of her dying children, sprinting to the edge of the conflict. "How?! How did they turn the battle around so swiftly?!" She stepped through flames and debris, gazing down at her lifeless offspring. Their twisted, bare muscle bodies were ridden with tears and gashes, lined with purple blood.

"Astonishing how the strength of an army doubles when its leader is at its front." Mocked a strong masculine voice.

"You? No, I watched you die." Lilith hissed with demonic presence. The figure that stood before her, with a raging fiery backdrop, grasped his swords leather bound handle tight, while in the other hand, he cradled the severed head of a hellish foot soldier.

"I remember seeing you, twice actually." The figure recalled.

Lilith winced with a potent mix of anger and befuddlement.

"Once, just as the world was fading from my sight, but I knew I recognised you from somewhere." He tossed the skull, it rolled to her feet. He approached her bravely. "Do you remember twelve years ago, that young man who in the heat of battle gave you a, somewhat, untraditional haircut."

"What of him? I killed him where he stood, filling his body with fire."

The figure grinned in response as its face gradually appeared from the shade. He did not respond, he merely waved.

Liliths' eyes shot open wider, as soon as she remembered his cheesy grin. "You bastard, how did you survive such magic?" Her hair began to flail as her muscles tightened, creating unappealing creases across her arms and legs.

"Before I left the city for that assault, the Prodigy Child blessed my armour on behalf of the Prophets."

Lilith snarled. She detested the thought of being bettered by a human.

"Please, give yourself some credit, you failed to take my life but you did rid me of half my vital organs and an awful lot of muscle tissue." He bowed sarcastically, an arm outstretched and the other folded at his stomach.

"And what of this occasion? How did you survive?" Gorton intervened.

"Ah I almost forgot about you. The men had warned me of your change of heart. Although…" He turned his head to Lilith. "You are not the only one who seems to have a change of heart over time."

"End your riddles human and answer me."

Lilith shied away, not wanting the conversation to continue.

"I have three things to say before I behead the both of you." He stomped down on another lifeless devil. "First of all." He held up a single finger. "Human? Yes it is what I am, but you should still address me as Commander. Second, I have no valid answer for your question, as I do not owe you an explanation. And finally…" He held up his final finger. "Do you know why we went to War with the Demon that takes your side, Gorton?"

"We started this War because the Kings safety was at risk, of course."

"Ah good, you remembered my lie." Once again, he grinned.

"Speak the truth dammit man!" Gorton ordered. Lilith remained motionless and speechless.

"The true reason this conflict started, is that thirteen years ago, I refused Lilith's advances. I cannot blame you for buckling to her though, she truly is exquisite." Again, the Commander tried his hand at talking down to them both.

"Seriously now Brekos, that kind of talk is hardly perceived as professional." Gorton replied, shrugging off his aching heart.

The Commander lowered his arms, they dangled limply by his side. He stared at them both lazily, an expression of boredom masked him. He paused, staring in silence as though he was disappointed with the reaction he received.

"…Excellent kisser too." He finally mumbled.

Gorton felt something inside him snap, like something he cherished as his own had been stripped from his life entirely. He made a fist, coping with the physical pain in his chest, standing became a chore.

"Brekos! You bastard!" He growled, diving towards his former brother. He swung his arms, swiping for Brekos in a blind rage. Regardless of the fact that all his attempts failed, he continued his assault, leaping after an agile human. His body too became ripped as his muscles bulged, just as Liliths' had when she was aggravated.

"All my serving days I have had to stand by as you constantly reached new heights! Always surpassing me! Always leaving me in your shadow!" He screamed as he launched himself over and over. "But this is where those days end! I am above you in every conceivable manner, and you will fall!"

Gorton attacked with all of his rage and strength focused into his fist. It blistered through the air, howling as it hurdled towards a defenceless Brekos. The jagged knuckles made impact, striking him with such force that the rock around them shattered, dust kicked from the ground.

Lilith stood in awe, swamped in fear, whereas Gorton finally felt as though he had taken the lead. However, his eyes then adjusted from the shockwave. He began to tremble, desperately wishing his eyes were lying.

"What…what have you done?" He stuttered. "What have you become?!"

Brekos was as sturdy as stone, his arm outstretched. His right hand was wrapped tightly around the fist, his fingertips gently pulling at Gortons' bruised flesh. His eyes were closed, his head slightly tilted towards the ground. He was calm.

"If I am correct Gorton, you called me a Human." His voice was coated with a silky, gentle echo as his eyes opened. "And that is what I am, by birth at the least…"

"What, the, hell?!" Gorton tugged, trying to free his shattered hand.

"Twelve years ago when your bride sent me to deaths door, Wrath was still free and held sympathy and hope for man."

"Why bring him into this?" snarled Gorton.

"I bring him into this because he saved my life!" A furious burst of light shuddered from his being, quickly fading into nothing more than a glowing outline. "He stripped part of his soul and gave it to me, to keep me alive, to keep me fighting the enemy which drove him to help me."

"That's a lie!" Squawked a still shaking Lilith. "He couldn't have given you his power! He was stripped of it when the Gods exiled him!"

"No Lilith he was not. His powers were not removed, merely restricted, making it impossible for him to access them through his own body. And so I act on his behalf, as the guardian of Hereteas. I will protect it from both man and demon, regardless of my connection to them." The light began to return, with a similar personality to the aura that surrounded Hermes, only Brekos possessed a white aura.

"There is no hope for you here." Grinned Gorton. "I am in an entirely different class to your own. What possibly makes you think you can succeed?"

The two demons began to laugh loudly with false victory.

"I can prevail, because I still stand." His eyes closed once again. The King and Queen halted their outburst and stared at the Commander, with a gaze of misunderstanding. "And until my last dying breath, as long as I can battle on..." The ground began to shake, pebbles springing to and fro. "...His will be done."

His words held such presence, such authority, that the battle seemed to soften, if only for a moment. Once more, his eyes opened, however this time, his irises were shining with a godly sea of light. In a single instant, he opened his hand, his palm flat against four broken fingers. A tiny spot of pressure surged at his hand, quickly exploding. Gorton flew through the air, thundering out of sight. The ground split and crumbled, forming a long derelict line before Brekos. Limp bodies were thrown to the side, some tumbling over the cliff and down into the icy sea.

His armour split, it dropped from his arms and torso in shards of steel and leather. His perfect muscular figure was revealed, though, at his navel, grew a small yet distinct burn. He ignored it, turning his head to Lilith. She was not afraid, only astonished and shocked at the power Brekos possessed.

Regardless, she did not speak or move. He raised his arm, aiming the tip of the blade at her neck from a distance.

"And his will is that this ends here tonight. That means you will not live to see another victim fall to your armies, Lilith."

# Chapter V

-

# Intuition

"Wrath, please, you have to help him." Gabriella pleaded. "No no that sounds far too needy." She paused to think. "Wrath, he will die without you. Hmm no still not appealing enough. Wrath, just think of what you can achieve together. The God and the Prodigy Child, side by side, vanquishing the scum of the land." She whipped her arm into the air, childishly rehearsing, stood to the side of the tunnels mouth.

"You know, I can hear you." Echoed a humoured voice.

Gabriella froze with embarrassment. She peeped her head around the corner before shuffling into the tunnel, staring at the ground, afraid to make eye contact with the former God. She stopped as she reached the mound of rubble, surrounded by puddles of melted ice. She caught a glimmer of her reflection, she hadn't realised how red she had turned, feeling foolish for practicing her proposal.

"Erm...Lord Wrath, sir, it would mean a great deal to me if you would accompany my fiancé in this battle." She actually asked, regretting how sloppy it sounded.

"You're fiancé? You mean Vixrol and yourself are due to be married?" Wrath replied, astonished.

"Yes sir that is correct. We are to wed in the Autumn."

"I highly doubt that. I am aware of your little spat earlier, and in brutal honesty, they sounded like parting words." He informed, aware that his words would be hurtful.

Gabriella smiled at her reflection, sweetly, partially agreeing with his comment. "The thing is my Lord, that there is much more to the human heart than meets the eye, that is why no one is aware of our engagement, because as I am sure you are aware, I used to be a beggar not so long ago. Others would simply not accept his judgement in this matter."

¬

"I must admit you have me there, I cannot think of a way to summarise the human heart and mind. However…" The pause in his words was filled with the scraping of chains as he arose from the corner near the window. "…I am also puzzled as to why you don't feel a need to question my knowledge of your argument with Vixrol."

"Oh, that is simple sir, I know all about your ability to see through the eyes of the few who are truly innocent." She raised her head, still wearing a smile, her eyes slightly teary from the harsh truth she had been presented with. "That's how you know about his exile right? Because you could see through the eyes of Brekos?"

"How could you know these things?" The almighty Wrath was startled.

"I'm not sure if I am permitted to tell you, but for now, let's just call it women's intuition." She giggled, folding her hands at the waist, adding to her innocence.

"There is very little that I overlook, but I will be keeping a close eye on you from now on, I can promise you that." For once Wrath was engaged in playful conversation.

"So erm…listen Wrath." She stuttered as she slipped some strands of hair behind her ear, which had fallen from her bun. "I know what you did, to be locked in here, and what you did is unforgivable."

Wrath stiffened with a growing anger, anger that he felt whenever his sins were brought to light.

"But I always believe that a man deserves to redeem himself, regardless of what he has done wrong. Brekos for example. Before the beasts of evil started to enter our land, he slaughtered hundreds of men, women and even children. Yet you found it within yourself to return his life to him." Her head started to sink a little lower with each word. "A life that surpassed his natural one. I do not know what capabilities he has now, but I do know that he borders on the realm of Gods. And…I just…" She began to weep, her mind wandering to dark subjects. "…I just don't want to see Vixrol buried before his time. And I know you can save him, I know you can."

"Gabriella…" His rage settled as sympathy overcame him. "…I am trapped in here, and as such all I can do it watch over him."

"If I free you please make sure he comes home!" She pleaded in emotional outburst. Wrath was speechless, no one had talked to him like this for years, and no one had needed him this way. He exhaled with deep regret.

"My lady…even if I was able to fight by him, I cannot fight as a God. I am a Human now and that's the unfortunate truth of the matter."

Yet another silence filled the room as Wrath walked towards Gabriella, though he was quickly reminded of his restraints as his metal cuffs ran out of leash.

"What if I could return your powers?" She suggested hesitantly.

"That isn't a possibility here. Only the Gods can release my restrictions."

"Yes that may be true but I think I know a way to at least bend your limits…"

"You speak of magic?" Again he found himself lost for words at such an offer.

"No, not as such. If you give me your word, that if I free you here and now, you must ride out immediately and find Vixrol and don't let him out of your sight until he is back in mine, then you will once again be feared by your enemies." She looked up at him, deep in his eyes, serious about her demand. "Just tell me what to do." A tear tumbled down her face, clinging to her chin before dripping away.

Wrath was taken back, for years he had imagined this moment, however he always imagined the King calling on his assistance, not a fragile young woman acting out of passion. He was about to be delivered his freedom, he felt as though he should be grinning insanely, but he knew what the future held.

"If you release me, you know that the King will have your head?"

"I do not care, I just want Vixrol to live."

"Then, if you are sure, all you have to do is want me to be free, and express it."

Gabriella stood tall, clenching her hands by her sides, she took a deep breath, preparing to sign away her own life. "Wrath…God of the burning cosmos and guardian of all mankind on Earth, I beg of you…"

The chains began to float around Wraths' arms, glowing a glorious golden shade.

"…Please deliver Vixrol to me, and keep your word."

"I swear on my soul, he will be returned to you, unharmed." He promised, shimmering steel cables surrounding him.

"Then I grant you your freedom."

Wraths eyes rolled back slightly, before his head drooped to his chest, as if he were unconscious. He remained standing. The illumination from the chains began to dim, then it stopped completely, and as

48

quickly as they had become a sight to behold, they turned back into average chains, dangling from his grubby body.

"Did…did it work?" queried Gabriella.

He did not reply. His face shielded by his greasy hair, just as it was when he met with Vixrol.

"Wrath is everything al-" Her sentence was cut short as she noticed the dirt running from his body. It moved like a thin wave, leaving behind smooth, clean, stainless skin. It trickled down his thighs and to his shins, creating an expanding cloudy puddle. Just as the edge of the muck reached his toes, his hair too began to drip. Oily goo dripped to the floor, his hair softening from the roots outwards. Though something about it was different, it wasn't just becoming clean, it was becoming shorter. The tip receded from the top of his abdomen, shrinking up to the base of his neck.

Gabriella was shocked at how dazzling he appeared, free of dirt and wearing his new look. Her jaw dropped ever so slightly, though her eyes widened. A loud rattle bounced through the tunnel, causing her to flinch. Her attention was once again drawn to his bare feet. The puddle was accompanied by reams of stretched and distorted metal links.

Wrath, still facing the ground, cautiously moved his arms from behind his back, for the first time in years. He opened his fists, to gaze at his palms. The last few bruises and sores, caused by his shackles, healed over, leaving a completely flawless being.

Turning his head up, he looked towards his saviour, but he gazed straight past her, down to the mouth of the tunnel and beyond. Drops of settled rain fell across the magnificent view of freedom. The puddles of dirt parted, avoiding his feet as he stepped towards the outside world, hesitant that he was once again trapped in his imagination, just as he had been many times before.

Step after step, the horizon was brought a little closer. He passed Gabriella as if she wasn't even there. His feet were graced with the refreshing kiss of water, and his skin was caressed by a gentle wind, as he exited his cell.

Straightening his back, he inhaled deeply, smiling at the familiar scent of summer, a welcome contrast to mould and infected wounds. A sudden, harsh breeze flicked his hair from his face, changing his loose, hanging style into softly spiked layers. It seemed to almost freeze that way, despite the wind stopping.

"Why has your appearance changed in such a way?" She asked, following him out of the darkness.

"This is my natural display. I always looked this way before I was sealed away." He smiled, happily, his eyes fixed on the fantastic view of plant life and manmade structures, blending together seamlessly. He ventured out of the Chapel, striding down the stairs. Streams of sunlight broke through the drifting clouds, greeting his person once again. "This is what I have missed, the reach of my creations."

"I'm sorry?"

"Remember, I am the creator of stars." He turned his head to Gabriella, who was stood by him. "And don't forget that I also created this Sun of yours."
"True, but that was a long time ago."

Wrath thought it was an odd comment for her to make, and he also felt as though he had been there before, standing by a gorgeous young woman, looking out across an entire civilization. He chose to ignore both these things, too overjoyed with the knowledge that he was free.

Suddenly there was a huge crashing boom, ripping through the peaceful atmosphere, bringing Wraths thoughts back to the situation. They both turned, protecting their vision from rubble as it hurdled towards them, followed by streams of dust. The room that had been Wraths home crumbled to the ground with huge bellows of smoke. The pavement cracked and split into large shards of rock. As the fractures reached the pillars of the Chapel, they began to climb, splitting and creaking their way to the roof.

In one quick swoop, Wrath tucked Gabriella under his arm, bounding down the steps towards the City. His heels did not touch the ground as he leant into his sprint, springing from his toes with impressive speed. Back at the scene of destruction, the pillars withered and burst under the structures weight, sending the shattered ceiling rolling down the steps, swiftly approaching the fleeing couple.

In an attempt to analyse the danger, Wrath leaped into the air, shuffling the maiden into a bridal carry grasp, holding her tight to his chest. As he spun himself around, he realised how desperate their predicament was. The rubble was almost upon them, and by the time they reached the city, they would be under it. If Wrath was alone, he knew he would walk away from such an impact with merely a scratch. However, with Gabriella in his arms, she would be crushed by the force, and her bones would not be able to withstand the pressure if he were to sprint at his best.

He whipped himself back around to face the city, using his leg as leverage. To brace for the landing, he raised his legs slightly, bending his knees, as if he were squatting. The ragged sheet of cloth that he wore slid between his legs, showing his bulging thighs. The tumbling roar of the boulders was joined by screaming civilians, aware of the tragedy that was about to unfold. Wraths heart suddenly hardened with the knowledge that once again, he would be unable to save them. It seemed like yet another day when the many would suffer for the few.

A small crater was formed as his feet buried into the ground, bricks and cobbled stone kicked into the air. Residences were knocked back by the aftershock. Wraths forearms skimmed the street as he slipped his arms from under Gabriella, leaving her lying beneath him. He let out a bellow as he swung his arms out straight, preparing for the rubble to strike. His eyes closed. Giving in to instinct, Gabriella curled into a ball, her arms wrapped around her head.

They both waited in fear as the ground trembled, a clear sign of the demolished structure approaching. The trembling continued, yet there was no impact. Wrath didn't take the risk, he stayed as he was, defending the woman who freed him. The screaming died away and changed to undefinable gossip and awe.

"Wrath, look." Gabrielle encouraged.

Reluctantly, he let his guard down to turn his head, just enough to see why he hadn't been hit. He found it hard to believe, but the rubble was piling up, leaning against what seemed like thin air, as if an invisible dome was covering the edge of the City. A cloudy, webbed pattern flickered across the field, giving Wrath some piece of mind.

"I recognise this barrier." He said as he stood back up.

"You've seen this phenomenon before?" Gabriella asked as she too began to stand.

"This isn't a phenomenon, miracle, or anything of the sort."

"Then…what is it?"

"Let us just say that I am about to become very temperamental." He warned as he examined the damage he had caused, pulling his feet from the dirt.

"You realise that doesn't help me at all don't you?" She smirked, disappointed.

"Then perhaps I can be of some assistance!" Cried a voice from the top of the towering rubble.

"Here we go…" Whispered Wrath under his breath.

The attention of all those present was drawn to the man standing above them.

"He's an Angel!" proclaimed a civilian.

"No! He is an illusion!" Contradicted another.

"A bastard is what he is." Again, he said to himself.

"Who are you?" Queried the maiden.

"I am the Fourth Original, Hermes!" The man announced, haloed by the scorching sun.

"What are you doing here Hermes? You know it is illegal to interfere in this realm." Wrath informed.

"Yes this is true, but where you are involved, it is my duty to ensure you are kept in check and follow this world's law."

"You confuse me brother. Last we met you shed a tear on my behalf, and yet here you are trying to kill me. Why?"

"My tears were of envy brother, not of sorrow."

"Envy?" Wrath exclaimed in uncertain surprise. "What is it I possessed that you envy? An insect has more luxury than I."

"It cripples me to know that scum like you need not be ruled by the First, yet I, a God, must constantly bow to his every demand."

54

"You speak of our brother as if he were an inconvenience. If he is listening, he will not heed your words with tolerance." A grin managed to creep through his solid expression, knowing that even Hermes shivered at the idea of confronting the First.

"As the God of Balance, I assure you he has more pressing matters than keeping his watch on me."

"Reasonable answer, but that doesn't explain why you just demolished what these people consider sacred."

"Oh, you'll have to forgive me, descending from our realm is usually rather powerful business and hard to control. Though it has been many years since you last experienced it, perhaps you have forgotten?" Hermes mocked, slowly hovering from his perch.

"Do not push me, boy."

"Yes, yes of course. Who would willingly aggravate the Third Original, renowned for his catastrophic powers and his unmatchable physical strength."

Wrath gave a brief shudder of anger, knowing that at his current stage, Hermes was an enormous foe, capable of completely destroying him.

"However, let us put that aside for a moment." Hermes decided, landing silently, his robes continuously dancing. "The King and I had an agreement to keep you imprisoned, he was to supply the cell, and I was to supply the enforcement. Although since you no longer have a cell, I can only assume that it is now my turn."

A manic grin spread across his face as he boomed with a dense aura, repelling the ruins he had suspended. They launched and rolled across the hill, upon which they came. His presence, once perceived as holy and divine, warped into a wicked, evil feel. The sky clouded over. Thick, black storm clouds rolled across the world, sinking it into shadow.

"Wrath! We have to go! Now!" Gabriella tugged at his wrist for him to follow her, yet he refused.

"I have yet to turn my back on a challenge, this is no different. I have an alternative. Why don't you fulfil your side of the bargain, and then I shall keep mine." Finally his eyes shifted from his nemesis to his saviour. "Return my powers to me, as he is a God he can easily kill me and then who would return your lover to you?"

She froze with heartache, realising that he was right. Her arms dropped from his hand as her head hung. She did not cry, she didn't even sob.

"Wrath...there should be a stallion near my quarters. He is one of the Kings finest. I want you to take him, and go after Vixrol. Leave here at once."

"I will do no such thing."

"That is an order!" She exclaimed quickly, shushing him. "Unless you do this, your powers will be forever out of reach."

"We had an agreement, woman." He turned his back to Hermes, more concerned that he had been fooled.

56

"What's wrong, human?! Do you realise that you are now as good as dead?!" Hermes interjected, grabbing Wraths attention once more. "You will wish that you never left your prison."

"He's right Wrath. Unless you leave, you will die, and this entire world will end with you. Or, you can redeem yourself and save it." Gabriella proposed, trying to get Wraths eyes to meet hers.

"Fine, I will go." He decided, rational though being difficult to find. "But first I have just one question for Hermes." He turned to see him. "Hermes! Why did you stop the rocks from landing?"

"We may not be permitted to interfere with mankind but if we are present in this word, and it is within reason, we are bound to protect them!"

"I see, now that's interesting." His attention switched towards Gabriella for a moment, before he turned and walked away.

"Where are you going!? Coward!"

"Forgive me Hermes, but this is out of my control, I swore an oath and I cannot die until it is fulfilled."

"So… you know you will die today." His voice trembled under his own power.

"Would you rather be known as Hermes, the God who killed a man, or as the God who slayed the Third?"

Hermes was shocked at Wraths submission. His raging light settled slightly as he found himself lost for words.

"That is what I expected." Wrath concluded.

Not another word was uttered as Wrath darted into the city, out of sight, in search of the horse he would ride. The battlefield shrank into the distance, as he left Hermes, and Gabriella behind.

# Chapter VI
-
# Touch of an Angel

The sky darkened as night once again coated the land. As he rode across the wasteland, emerging from the maze of ruins and forestation, Wraths attention was drawn above. He looked up to the stars, for the first time in years, hypnotised by his creations. They twinkled in a cloudless vision of beauty, shining down on him from afar. He could not help but smile as his hands relaxed on the reins. It was an unusual feeling he noticed, as he was miles from anyone who could judge him. He once again felt as though he was worth something, like the cosmos needed him and his place in it was unshakable.

"As much as my heart yearns to stay here, I must not forget my objective." He looked down at the steeds bobbing head as he galloped with all his strength. "You seem tired, my friend." Wrath said as he noticed the horses heavy panting.

Suddenly, the panting and clicking of hooves was dimmed by a thunderous roar, one that sent shivers through both of their spines. Wrath glanced over his shoulder, tightening his grip on the leather straps. They were being followed, by an ink like stream of gold, soaring across the sky. It moved with incredible pace, much faster than the horse could travel.

"Dammit. Sorry but this might feel a little unusual, just focus on running." Wrath commanded, placing a hand flat between the horses shoulders, the strap wrapped around it to keep him stable. On his forearm, he rested his other hand, squinting down. "Brothers on high, hear my call. Share my gift with this creature so that I may charge my enemies or escape my foes. I beg of thee, give his soul my wings!"

The stallion whinnied in discomfort as shards of blue and green light pierced its back, leaving no scars as they entered. Their purpose was very quickly made apparent as the speed of its gallop rocketed, its mane pinned back by the wind. Wrath tucked himself close to the horses back, stiffening to prevent a fall. The brittle, mousy brown fur bleached into a pearly white coat. The colour bled out like a thick, mystical oil, dripping and rolling behind them both, acting like a detached cape. Its once glossy mane and tail burst into glorious white flames, with the occasional sliver of green.

"Alright Hermes, let's do this!" Wrath called, rising from his tucked position, the wind whistling by his neck. As soon as his challenge was announced, another loud clash blistered across the land as Hermes once again increasing his velocity. His golden trail grew thicker and longer as it twisted and rippled towards its target.

Realising that his enemy was now on the offensive, Wrath whipped his arm into the air, his fingers tensed in a claw-like fashion. In an unexpected dash, the oily dye, tumbling behind them, zoomed upwards, swallowing the yellow flash, extinguishing it as it tumbled to the rocky dirt. The liquid bulged and warped as it struggled to contain the God. Wrath turned back around, grinning at his victory.

As his eyes focused, despite the crippling momentum, he noticed a small figure in the distance.

"Vixrol!" He bellowed in relief that he had reached him before he had come to any harm. "Gabriella sent me!"

The figure made no attempt to turn or respond, it just slowly paced away.

"Don't test me boy, I'm here to help you!"

Due to the formidable pace of the Godly steed, Wrath was by the figure in no time at all. It was Vixrol, undoubtedly, right down to the mark on his arm. Wrath slowed the horse to a steady trot.

"Vixrol? What in the Hell are you doing?" He became concerned at the soldiers zombie like motions and total ignorance. He reached down and placed a hand firmly on his shoulder, halting his pace. "Vixrol what happened? Say something before you begin to frustrate me."

Slowly, and with an unsettling abandon of emotion, Vixrol finally turned to his company. There was something different about him, he wasn't the brave young warrior who darted from the cell, when they previously met. His eyes were closed and his actions were lazy, as though he were unconscious.

"You…" He mumbled with drunken effort. "You should not be here…"

61

"I already explained, your fiancée sent me to protect you." Wrath comforted, resisting the urge to make his strength as a free man clear.

"You...killed them..."

His words tightened a knot in Wraths stomach, one which would not be forgiven lightly. He removed his hand from the zombies shoulder and rested it on the blazing steeds flank. With a controlled and calm swing of his leg, he dismounted, crouching as he landed, sinking so his head was level with Vixrols belt. In a burst of anger he launched upwards, seizing the man by the throat, lifting him into the cool night air. Tall and strong, Wrath asserted his dominance.

"You will regret your words, Human. I am no longer bound by physical restraints, ripping you apart would be a much needed warm up." His words oozed with promise and pain at the memory of his failures.

"Daddy why won't the God man save us? He will darling just wait, he will come." Vixrols voice shifted into the different characters, a small girl to a frightened man, unfazed by his buckling neck.

Wrath was taken back, the faces of dying innocent people flashing before his mind. Their cries for help, screams of pain, the silence after the event, it rang clear as day. His eyes quivered in horror.

"And yet, the God man never came. He just watched as they all went down, down, down." Again, he mocked like a child singing a nursery rhyme.

Wraths grip tightened as his yellow eyes shimmered with creeping tears. His free hand switched from a fist to an open position, wanting to beat Vixrol, however swallowed by regret, he was finding it hard enough just to remain standing. Vixrols eyes slowly eased open, bloodshot and teary, they were the only real evidence that he was choking. Wraths lips parted, though his teeth were grinding.

"Down…down….dow-"

With a cry of despair, Wrath brought his arm back, closing his eyes as shaking his head. In a fierce thrust he crashed the tease into the ground. Despite being blinded by a huge rush of dust and sand, kicked up as the rock split, he was able to feel Vixrols adams apple collapse under the pressure. A quiet whimper escaped as he hung his head, fighting back any evidence of sorrow.

"I'm sorry Gabriella. I just couldn't let him talk in such a way. Not about that. Not with me." A single salty bead trickled through his eyelids and dripped to the ground.

"Why…?" Asked a sweet voice through the dust.

Wraths eyes shot open in confusion, only to be confronted with a familiar face, splattered with rubble and blood.

63

"Gabri...Gabriel-"

"Why did you kill him Wrath?" Streams poured from her eyes, carving away the blood on her cheeks. "You lied to me, you promised Wrath. You promised."

Wrath ripped his hand from the mangled neck, stepping back, genuinely frightened and lost.

"What is this? You were...no...." He looked on in dismay as the crippled woman stumbled to her feet, her head swinging like a ball on a string.

"You killed him Wrath, my love, the man you were sent to protect. You're a monster and you always will be."

"Gabriella no, I did what I had to. If he were permitted to continue, my rage for him would grow with each passing second." He clenched his fists as he summoned the courage to approach her shuffling body.

"Temper, temper Wrath." Her head swung back just in time for him to catch a glimpse of a wicked grin. His rage once again flared, and once again, he surrendered to its will. He drove his fist into the corpses gut, piercing straight through. His front leg bent, his back stretched and stiff, his form perfect. He found himself looking past the body as it firmly cuddled his arm.

"Now you can join your lover in Hell." As quickly as his anger boomed, it settled.

"Is that truly a way for a God to act?" Quizzed yet another familiar voice.

Wrath winced at the question. "Brekos, please, not you too." He begged, standing upright beside the figure.

"Ah, so your memory still hasn't faltered these past years, I'm impressed."

Wrath looked down and to his satisfaction, his arm was not in the belly of his friend. Instead, it was tightly clamped by one of Brekos's mighty arms.

"I see you have found a use for my gift to you." He stated as he noticed the small burn spreading from his abdomen.

"Not so much a need, just the occasion." Brekos protected, releasing the former Gods arm and backing away slightly. The burn began to grow rapidly, skin blistering and peeling away in its wake. "I am not here to mock or frustrate you, I am here for my own reasons."

"And what reasons would you be referring to?" Wrath began to pace around the Commander cautiously.

"I have come to say goodbye."

"So, you truly intend to do my will?"

"That is what I swore to you, and as we speak I am engaging a new, powerful enemy."

"I am aware, Gorton, am I right?"

"Indeed." He bowed his head with mild disappointment at his once good Captain. "Although your gift directly links me to you, and from what I can tell, you need nothing more now than an old friends help."

"You always were good at judging people Brekos." Wrath chuckled, nudging Brekos with his elbow.

"Haha, all except Gorton it seems. Wrath listen." His tone became serious. "This body is not my own and I very much hated the idea of controlling that steed of yours, so there is little time for me to say what I need to, so please, listen."

Wrath centred his attention on his friend. "Speak Brekos."

"The time of the Prodigy Child is an eternity of wait away, though for you it will be little more than a Cycle."

"Brekos your words make no sense."

"They will very soon." He nodded. "As I ascended to the realm of Angel I could see everything. I know the path you will walk and I know the road you will choose." He raised a hand and gripped Wraths firm shoulder, rocking him like an old friend would. Wrath turned his head to ensure the hand was unarmed. It was, though the burn had already reached his wrist. "You were once worshiped as one of the greatest of the Original Eight. You are a fine God Wrath, but even more than that, you....."

The kind words suddenly silenced. Wrath looked up from the hand in curiosity.

"But you are out of luck, brother." Warned Hermes, slipping his hand to the front of his brothers' shoulder, snapping his long narrow fingers through Wraths flesh. He wrapped them around his collar bone, fracturing it with his immense strength. Wrath pressed towards Hermes, trying to ease the pressure on his collar. However Hermes had always felt uneasy in the presence of the Third, let alone when he was no longer chained. Because of this, he quickly put distance between himself and his fallen relative.

With a crazed smile he raised one leg and planted his foot deep into Wraths stomach, lifting him from his feet and launching him across the plain before he crashed to the ground. The clash of the strike startled the stallion, causing it to blaze into the distance. Hermes let out a laugh of insanity, gripping a sizable chunk of splintered bone in his fist.

"What's this?! The great immortal Wrath being mutilated with such ease? Who knew!" He slowly paced towards his crippled rival, who was writhing on the stone, clutching his shoulder in inexpressible agony. "I never thought you would sink so low as to leave a woman to fight your battle for you, while you fled like a coward. That was definitely something new."

Wrath struggled to think straight, his nervous system going haywire, never before experiencing such pain. "Gabriella…what did you do to her?" He murmured, blood creeping through his fingers.

"Me? What did I do to her? That bitch gave me more trouble than I care to admit, it seems as though someone is looking out for her at least."

"Did you hurt her?" Wrath questioned as his foe stood over him.

"I'm sorry did I what?" Hermes pressed immaturely.

"Did you hurt her?!" He managed to raise from the dirt a little, though he quickly lay back, pinned by his injury.

"Oh yes I thought that is what you said. Simply put, no I didn't hurt her."

"Thank you." He sighed, tilting he head back and squinting in pain.

Hermes turned and began to walk away. "However...I guess it depends on your perspective. Tell me wrath..." He turned once again to face the bloody heap of a God. "Would you consider having your womb ripped from your body painful?"

A sinister chill darted through Wraths body, so cruel that his heart seemed to stop. He felt more horrified at the injury Hermes suggested than at the idea of killing Gabriella himself. A lack of control unsettled him.

"I mean think about it for a minute, not only is it a life ending injury, but even if she were to survive, what use would she be to any man now? Perhaps to Vixrol for example..." His words were of pure evil and bloodlust, shattering heart for the mere sport of it.

Wrath mustered all the strength he could just to roll to his knees, it took even more for him to struggle to an untidy, hindered stance. "Our brothers will not forgive you for this act of heresy…" His muscles tensed and his voice deepened into a slight growl. "To wound a human is an absolute breach of the law."

"Oh please do not concern yourself with my punishment, it seems as though a being outside of the Eight took it upon herself to make my sins apparent." He tweaked the neck of his robes, slipping it down to reveal a fresh, splitting scar.

"How? How could a being outside of us cause such a thing?" His muscles continued to bulge. "To wound a God you must either be a Demon, Angel or a-"

"A God? Yes perhaps you are correct. Still, the damage is rather impressive considering it was dealt by the hand of a Second Generation God." He said, admiring his torn skin.

Once again Wrath fell into silence, not out of pain, not out of anger, but out of pure amazement. "She…did this?"

"Her identity was unmistakeable. At her birth she was stripped of any connection to her divine heritage. Though it seems no matter how much she loses, there is one thing that we cannot take from her." Hermes looked down at his victims bowing face. "And if you get anymore enraged, you will end up using the same method as her to kill me."

"Hermes, let us set our dispute aside, just for a moment." Wrath pleaded as another burst of blood spewed from his chest.

"A moment is all I shall grant."

"Did she look well? Did she seem healthy as a human?"

"Wrath she was berserk. Regardless of how 'well' she may look, during that stage of survival it is a terrifying sight, I assure you." His words were not of taunt or sarcasm as he pointed a bloody finger, he was regrettably serious as he expressed his fear.

"And you killed her...?" snarled Wrath.

"Actually I was unable to land a single blow, the only reason I left was to make sure you did not reach the battlefield."

Wrath smiled. "Yes because even you know better than to confront an Angel, let alone one of my creation."

"I believe you have had your moment..." His face stiffened in insulted disgust. He heightened to his toes, before totally clearing the ground, hovering slightly above it. He began to drift back, his gown gracefully folding in the breeze. "You could have continued down a dark and lonely road, yet in an attempt to reach the light, you have condemned yourself to Hell for the rest of your Underlife." Hermes raised one arm, dropping the shard of bone, and faced his palm towards the hobbling state of a man, blessing him with an execution speech.

A faint yellow glow surrounded his palm. It thickened and expanded until it became a vortex of raw energy, spiralling and swirling. Thin whips of lightening danced around the God as his power increased, thundering and clashing, as though he himself had become the storm. "And if you ever crawl out of the pit of a realm…" His eyes blazed with yellow and orange ripples, shimmering in the night. "…I will wipe you from existence all together."

As the vortex swelled and thickened, preparing to fire, a whoosh of blistering mass darted past Wrath, the stallion returned and closed down on the enemy, a slim figure upon its back. All of its fur has smouldered and moulted, leaving scarred tissue and a fiery mane behind. In desperate frustration, Hermes cried out, enhancing the attacks progress. It was too little too late. The figure leapt into the sky as the long head of the horse crashed into the God, knocking the wind out of him, breaking his concentration and breaking his attack.

Wrath sheltered his head with his undamaged arm, knowing the event that would follow. He crouched to the ground and braced himself. In surreal manner, the horses' body expanded and began to bloat. Its skin started to rip apart. The gaps were replaced with dense, physical light, transforming the steed into an immense bomb.

With one final flash, it detonated, shaking the earth and tearing the landscape apart. A bellow of white smoke filled the sky as it rocketed from the source, decorated with green and blue highlights. No matter how powerful Hermes was, the animal had been blessed with Wraths soul, and as such, was in the realm of Gods.

The smoke steadily settled and drifted with the wind, creating luminous clouds across the starry backdrop. A burst of golden aura bloomed inside the dust, zooming up and out of sight. Hermes had retreated.

Wrath sat down and relaxed a little, since he was no longer under threat, he could examine his wound. It was deep and gaping. He felt scared, yet he accepted his emotions. Blood had stained his torso, neck and cloth, he was close to death.

"That looks like it hurts." Commented an innocent voice to his back.

He shuffled to catch a glimpse of his new visitor, praying that it would not be a foe.

"Man may not be able to kill you but I promise that unless you get that arm treated, you will die like any other Human would."

Wrath smiled with slight disbelief as he saw her, standing tall, a golden dress hanging loosely from her shoulder, hardly covering her breasts. Her locks seemed to match her uniform whereas her pale skin was a closer match to the crystal clouds that hung above them. Her shining yellow eyes gazed cheerfully into his.

"It is good to see you at last, Lailah."

# Chapter VII

-

# Body of Scars

A once beautiful, coastal scene had been transformed into a portrait of chaos. Tents were ablaze, bodies piled high, and the sky was shrouded with smoke. The pair darted around the battlefield, locked in combat. To mortal eyes, their speed could only be perceived as buzzing images of men as they clashed, before again vanishing to reappear elsewhere. The ground beneath them started to show signs of crumbling, miniature craters forming. The men did the best they could to catch a glimpse of their Commander, praying that he would be the victor. Unfortunately for them, the hordes of monsters showed little interest in the couple, hungry and searching for a fresh meal, keeping the humans preoccupied.

Gorton would often force his adversary towards his previous comrades, purposefully slicing them with his spiked, axe like arm. Finally the conflict between them halted for a brief moment as they skidded in opposite directions, gripping the dirt with bare toes.

"Seems as though crushing your arm back there was a mild mistake." Brekos suggested, raising his claymore to the sky. It glittered as power infused with the blade. Rubble peeled away from his place of standing.

"Actually I rather like its consequences." The demonic man contradicted, swinging his weaponised arm before pulling it back to his side, as though he would charge. "Though from what I can see, using that form is taking its toll on your body."

He was referring to the burn which quickly spread over his chest as Brekos pumped more energy into his blade. "Do not act so confident, devil, the power I am blessed with will be my death, but I will not die here alone." He assured as the colour in his eyes faded, from a cloudy white to a sunburst yellow.

His sword pulsed as it oozed with floating light, warping the air that touched it, the same way the blazing landscape was distorting the horizon.

"Ah good, you seem much more focused than before." Gorton praised.

"Forgive me, but I had something urgent I had to attend."

"HA! How pitiful, you've gone mad with fear Commander!" He screamed as his arm sprouted yet another pointed spine.

"Not quite." The Commander replied calmly as the sword exploded, holding all the energy it could. As the quick burst of smoke cleared from his weapon, it was clear to see that it was no longer of that realm. The hand guard had sprouted decorative steel wings, which circled and twirled around the base of the blade. It was huge, at least double the width it was previously. Its tip was sharpened with razors of light. Gorton squinted, knowing that the battle had just escalated once again.

"Darling, it isn't polite to play with your food!" Encouraged Lilith, sitting aloft a rock to the edge of the conflict, in the same position as she was when Gorton first saw her. He found her words comforting, after all, she gave him his powers, so surely she could foresee his potential.

He raised his mutated arm and leapt towards the shining warrior, releasing a battle cry mid-jump. As he prepared to swing his target disappeared. He hesitated and crunched to the ground, the ball of his foot ripping into it. Scanning the battlefield, his eyes darted back and forth, though no sign of his foe could be found. Suddenly, his vision was blocked by a splattering curtain of blood, spraying up. Pain flooded his body as he tilted his head down, a deep gash vomited blood violently, stretching from his left pectoral across to his right hip.

Despite his body burning, he heard a loud ripping noise. He swivelled on his toes to find its origin. To his surprise, he found Brekos standing, facing away. His arm was straightened across his chest, blood dripping down its length. As Groton examined the scene, he narrowed down the noises source. Flakes of dry, brittle skin drifted around the Angel, shedding from his back. Clearly using speed and accuracy such as that had cause equal damage to both parties.

Brekos's shoulder blades began to ripple and squirm, bruising over. He jabbed the blade into the dirt, supporting his weight on the hilt as he doubled over. A smile spread across Gortons' face, confident that his enemy had been damaged more than expected. With a burst of white mass, his confidence vanished and was replaced with fear.

.

Out of the Angels back, stood a huge set of dazzling pearly wings, hanging out and above the quaking Commander. He quietly focused, trying to ignore the crippling pain that engulfed him. His growing scar deepened, summoning speckles of blood to the surface.

Stiffening his brow and reminding himself of the task at hand, he sealed his lips in effort, ripping his weapon from the ground and turning to the wounded demon. The Angel, paralyzed in pain, the Demon, paralyzed in fear. They starred each other down in silence while the wails and cries of beast against man, littered the air.

"You boys bore me." Sighed the Queen, skipping from her rock and pacing away from the pair.

"My bride! Why do you leave?!" Gorton questioned, gripping his chest with his human hand.

"It's what she does. She will be here for the moment, but gone as soon as you need her."

"Silence you old fool!"

"The truth hurts you? He is correct Gorton, if you cannot keep me entertained then I have no need for you." Her words wounded him just as much as his physical abrasion.

Unwilling to lose yet another woman from his life, he cried out in desperate frustration. His yell grabbed her attention for a brief moment, enough to tweak the corners of her lips.

A lesser creature caught scent of an Angel on the wind, and in blind starvation, scurried towards him. Its forked tongue dangled from its mouth, drool flicking from it.

Gorton felt an unusual sense of instinct as his pupils shrank until they vanished and his irises faded away, leaving a set of bloodshot eyeballs. He rotated his human arm up, so his hand aligned with his shoulder. He paused. As the beast sprinted on all fours past him, his arm extended and stretched, his muscles pulling tight into a long, scrawny strand. The monster was sent grinding into the stone, fingertips smashed into its skull like a hook. It finally dragged to a stop, lifeless, its slobber now mixing with its blood into a clouded purple pool.

Brekos was puzzled and stunned, unsure as to why his enemy would be defending him. The lanky arm began to shorten, pulling the corpse with it. It started off steady, creeping back in, before whipping back to its normal state. The body hung like a farmyard animal after the slaughter, its feet resting on the ground, its sharp pointed toes curled.

Again the duelling pair was still, all apart from Brekos who had begun to pant with exhaustion as the burn continued to grow. Gorton quietly let out a long, chilling exhale, as though he were satisfied in some twisted way. His eyes started to cloud over with a pink haze as his chest rose up. Suddenly, without reason, both the Demon and his kill erupted into a sea of mixed blood. Their bones melted into a sloppy, clay-like material. Much blood had coated the ground during the war, but for some reason, this blood did not fall. It hovered and wandered around the air, like droplets in a vacuum. Threads of blood linked with one another, creating a vast map of waving red strings.

"What is this?" The shining being questioned, failing to raise his sword.

"Beautiful isn't it, the way it shimmers in the light." Lilith pondered, looking towards the liquid structure in awe.

"I don't understand…is he dead? Is it over?" A sense of hope filled his tone. If he had been victorious this early in his transformation, there was a slim chance that he could revert to a human and survive.

"Please Brekos, try not to be so dull. If he were dead…" She peered up at him from afar, strands of hair bordering her eyes. "…how is it that he has surpassed you?"

As her silver tongue finished waving, Brekos noticed rivers of blood, drifting from the main lot. They towered above him and dropped to his flank. He turned as swiftly as he could, only to see his enemy, swinging towards him. His body was forming out of the liquid, however thus far only his head, bust and a sharpened arm had been completed. His eyes glowed with white blazes, highlighting his tense, red brow. In an act of defence, Brekos tried to lift his blade above his head, to block the ambush. His injuries were taking a heavy

78

effect on him. He was unable to flinch, let alone lift the mighty sword from the ground. All he could do was brace for yet another blow.

The attack made contact, a rush of sparks dived into the air. It was unusual, abnormal, Brekos felt no pain, not even so much as the pressure of an impact. He turned his head a little more to see a pair of legs quivering behind him, the knees starting to buckle. He tried to see more of the body, however it was blocked by his feathered extensions. His body was aching, he couldn't move his wing to see the identity of his saviour. Regardless, he was certain that the one who intervened must be friend as opposed to foe.

He gripped his sword tightly, screaming in pain and torture as he forced himself to lift it. He shuffled his right leg behind the other, carrying the weapon to his left shoulder. His hips pivoted and his arms extended, swinging the blade full force towards his opponent, and his protector. Its glimmering edge sliced through them both, before its wielder crashed to the ground, wings slumped by his sides.

The Demon exploded once more into showers of blood, and this time, the swirling map collapsed along with it. The Angel rested on his palms, breathing heavily, too tired to even keep his eyes awake. They closed, blocking his glowing yellow irises from the world.

"What the Hell did you just do…?" Shivered a bewildered voice.

"You need not worry, if you are Human then this blade cannot harm you." The commander answered sleepily, raising his eyebrows, but unable to open his eyes.

"I am a man, but not much of one." It informed as it paced to the front of the grounded warrior.

"You just saved the life of a divine creature, I assure you, I wish I had ten thousand more like you." He winced as he started to recall how many men he had actually lost that day.

"Ten thousand like me? Words like that could lead the people of this land to overthrow you."

The Angel grew more curious of his guardian, and out of gratitude, pushed himself to his feet, using his wings as additional support. He finally stood up, though it went hand in hand with an ever growing burn. The blistered soles of his feet were cooled by the touch of icy cold blood from his vanquished adversary. His eyes flickered open unwillingly, and it took several moments to focus on the man before him.

"Dare I ask why a God is fighting to protect us?" The man asked with upset of betrayal.

Brekos's eyes adjusted, revealing the blooded face of the one who saved him. His beaded hair dripped with thick, red gunge. His knees continued to wobble, still suffering from the force of a demons attack. Battered, gleaming armour gripped against his athletic structure. While his eyes were fixed on the Commanders.

"Vixrol…?"

"You know my name, now tell me, which God are you? Tristen? Reaper?" He pressed his claymore again the Angels throat. "Or are you Wrath in your true form?"

With an insulted swing of his arm, Brekos knocked away the danger at his neck. "I'm no God you proud fool!"

"Then what are you?!" Vixrol questioned, recovering his stance after being slightly tossed.

"Brekos Eastartes!"

Vixrol back away slightly in disbelief. "No…no…the Commander is but a man."

"Before you joined my ranks, I was a Captain like you, at which time, Wrath divided his soul and gifted it to me. As such, I am in a realm between that of Man and the Eight."

"…Can I be honest Commander…" Vixrol queried, relaxing into the situation.

"By all means."

"I never expected this." He chuckled. His comment was quickly followed by a friendly smirk between the two, secretly happy to be fighting by one another again. Though the comforting moment did not last long. The chilling puddles at their feet smeared from under them, uniting into one large collection.

It grew upwards and gradually took on the basic form of a person. The soldiers prepared themselves for battle, Brekos still struggling with his injury.

"Commander, what is that?"

"That, Captain, is Gorton." Brekos informed.

"...Seriously, what the Hell did I miss?"

"Just as much as me. I was out cold for the whole thing."

"Care to explain?"

"Maybe later."

The Commander winced once again.

"Commander, you seem far too weak to fight. If you must, take a moment to rest, I am sure that my magic can distract him for the moment." As he offered his assistance, large folds of liquid spread from the shapes back, dripping and moulding into huge, bat-like wings. "On second thoughts sir, perhaps I may be a little outmatched."

"Oh, you think?" They seriously joked, using conversation as a fear reducing mechanism. Vixrol took a small step of retreat, offering Brekos the field. As he fell out of his superiors' vision, a slimy, spongy sensation surrounded his neck. It dragged him off balance, distancing his feet from the ground. He swung his arm franticly, trying to slice the vice around him. His weapon flew from his hand as he was hauled from his comrade. Gripping the snake like muscle, he pulled it away from his throat, allowing him to breathe, releasing a weak howl as he gasped.

"Vixrol!" The Commander screamed in concern, finally lifting his blade from the ground.

"Your fight is with me, Commander. Now please..." The demon raised its spilling head, revealing his lifeless eyes. "...Allow my bride to have her fun."

Meanwhile, Vixrol tumbled to the ground, rolling as the wet surface slipped from his person. He gasped for air, rubbing his neck to ensure he was not harmed.

"Mmm...I must say even for a Human you taste...delectable." Lilith announced, pacing around her catch, her serpent tongue skimming under her narrow chin and up her smooth jaw.

"I am not certain whether to be flattered or disgusted. Tell me..." He began, climbing to his feet, shuffling to a stable stance as he wiped a smudge of blood from under his nose, drawn from his landing. "...Who the fuck are you." He took personal offense to being touched by a woman in a manner such as this, resolved to keep his oath to his beloved Gabriella.

"Ah yes, I must apologise, I forgot you had been sent off before my grand entrance." She grinned.

"Still no closer to an answer..." Vixrol grew impatient.

"Fine, I shall skip the banter and get straight to my point." She placed a hand upon her hip and gestured with her other as she explained. "I am Lilith, the Sixth Original."

"Oh, so you are a God." He pointed.

"Not as such, I used to be but...well...an eternity is no fun unless you break the rules."

"I wouldn't know, unlike some I am blessed but not with an endless life."

"You are mistaken, we can absolutely be ended, but only by the hands of our own."

"I beg to differ, I am sure my Commander could drive you to the edge."

"Are you seeing a different scene to me? He is close to collapse and my King has practically brought an end to this boring game already."

"Well then, why don't I entertain you some?" He doubled over before flinging himself upright, lashing his arm as though to slap her up over. However his attack was not an assault, there was too much distance between them. Instead, a rod of ice lashed from his fingertips. It dangled at first, like a fibre, before stiffening into a glistening shard. As quickly as it appeared, his magic evaporated into glittering dust.

A slim cut opened along Liliths cheek.

"Getting interesting?"

She dabbed her fingers on her wound, examining the blood that stuck to them. "Hmm...not interesting as such, just slightly impressed." Her cheek sealed itself, strands of skin pulling the wound shut. "You didn't even speak the incantation."

"If you are impressed by that, then it would be wise not to aggravate me."

"Let's just see how that plays out." She challenged, lowering herself to a fighting stance.

Once again Vixrol manoeuvred his hand towards the Queen, and once again ice was summoned and propelled at her. Only this time she dodged swiftly, sweeping to her side in elegant motion. Suddenly she vanished, and did not reappear. A crushing blow plunged into Vixrols ribs, smashing them as he was sent thundering through the battleground. He tumbled through pillars of rock, clutching his torso as he bounced to a halt. He squirmed on the ground, writhing in agony, kicking his legs as though he was trying to escape his own body.

"Seriously? A knee to the ribs and the Prodigy Child is done for? You disappoint me." She had appeared again and was crouched by his head with her knees together.

"Tell me..." He coughed, blood spluttering over his face. "Do you know why I was chosen as the Prodigy Child?"

"Can't say I've heard the tale. Enlighten me."

"Ironic choice of words. I was chosen..." He coughed again, squeezing his side. "Chosen because I can instantly forge my own spells."

"Again, you fail to impress me."

He looked up into her eyes and smiled, clearing his throat.

"What lovely blue eyes you have..." She complimented, pondering whether to attempt to take this Captain as her King.

"Your eye isn't too bad either."

She looked at him puzzled at his bad use of speech. A spearing rip broke the silence, soon followed by the tapping of blood droplets. The dripping became a gush, running out onto her silky thighs.

"...Oh..."

"I'm glad you get my point."

She stood back up and traced her finger round her eye socket, her burst, flattened eyeball catching her fingers. She pulled it from her head and flicked it away.

"Forgive me but that truly is unpleasant." He quivered in disgust.

"May I ask how?"

"Even Gods have moisture in their eyes."

"You did it again..."She snarled.

"I'm sorry?"

"You called me a God. I told you..." She brought her left leg back. "I am not a God!" She boomed as she kicked him in the head, launching him yet again. The damage was much more serious than that delivered by her previous strike. His neck was shattered as he lay motionless amongst mounds of burning bodies. He could not feel any pain, and in so felt an odd sense of relief. This feeling died as soon as he caught sight of his enemy, elevated above him, a hand covering her gaping skull. "I had intended to let your path flow its course. Though your arrogance has just changed my mind." She lowered her hand, showing a pair of eyes, her missing one regenerated.

"As if I would allow my fate to assist you in any manner." He stung.

"On Deaths doorstep and still resilient. Shame." She drew her hand back. A dark grey fog formed in her palm, before it stretched into a lengthy thorn. "Any last words?"

"Just make sure you hit me where it counts."

"With pleasure." She aimed with her forward hand as her posture stiffened, preparing to project her weapon. In a single instant, a flick of time, her body snapped, hurdling the spear towards the crippled Captain. It flew with such force that the surrounding flames bowed away. It zoomed towards his head, centred with perfect accuracy. Yet, it stopped. The peak of the spike paused

87

between his eyes. He was alive. Then something did press against his brow. Blood trickled and dripped to his face, streaming into his inset creases. His gaze drifted the length of the thorn, the end of which was out of sight. It was blocked by a skinless figure, a large set of bald wings to either side, holes ripped through their flesh.

"Gorton...?" Vixrol muttered.

"I am afraid not, my Captain."

Vixrols eyes widened with painful truth, blood seeped into the folds in his eyelids. "Commander...why?"

"Listen to me Vixrol...the words I spoke to you earlier were not my own. You are one of the best men I have had the gracious gift of meeting throughout my life."

"How sweet, famous last words of a dying legend." Gorton spoke boldly to his Queen, who stood proud beside him in the air. His body was scarred and battered, though it did not faze him.

"Let us hear them." The Queen allowed.

"Commander please do not talk this way." The cripple begged.

"You must listen, Vixrol. My soul was divided between my own and the Thirds'. When you insulted me, his pride took over, creating a distance between my mind and body. Lilith was able to creep in and shut down my organs." He wretched blood as his strength faded. "That is what they waited for. They wanted you to live. You, can choose, Vixrol. Choose who wins this war. The light, or the darkness. We all want you to live my brother, including Wrath."

"Brekos...don't..." Tears swelled his eyes.

"When I am gone away, you must seek his council. He can be your greatest asset throughout your life. Use that."

"I think I may vomit. Hurry up and die you disgrace!"

"Not quite yet Gorton! There is one more thing you must deal with..."

"Get to the point! I grow tired of this."

"Aren't we all." Lilith agreed quietly.

"What do you think this burn represents?" Brekos questioned, looking up at them both with bloodshot, yellow eyes. His last remaining skin, the size of an eye patch, shrinking.

"It's beyond me, but you have grown weaker the larger that burn gets. I'd say it is a ticking countdown to your demise."

Brekos smiled, knowing that his enemy would come to that conclusion. He took a step forward, ripping the shard from his chest and tossing it away. "As soon as my body is nothing but a scar, I have one minute. One minute to kill you. That time is more than enough."

"You would succumb to one of our pets within moments in your current state. Your threat is meaningless."

"We will see..." He smiled in submission to his fate. "Vixrol, I am sorry that I was not able to put this battle to rest myself, I pass my torch to you." He turned to look down at the paralyzed soldier. "You will see that this ends, Commander Vixrol Decimus." Tears filled both the warriors' eyes, and several trickled down. "Farewell." He dropped his divine sword. It hit the dirt with a clang.

Vixrol tried to protest, until the lump in his throat choked him. He whimpered as he began to weep. His inspiration paced away, dragging his wings, a hole through his chest. He shuffled to the cliff before floating up to face his enemies. This skin around his eye had almost vanished.

"I'd say you have ten seconds to repent for your sins."

"And if we do not?" Lilith gloated.

"Then..." His final shred of skin peeled away. "...On your head be it." With his final words, his eyes clouded over from the edged, cleansing to a blank canvas. As he stared at his foes, a heavenly light emitted from his eyes. His hair and tattered clothes became weightless as they drifted around peacefully. A deep, animalistic snarl grumbled from him as the outer layers of his body vaporised, blowing away in a twinkling sea of particles.

Lilith became rigid, overcome with a familiar sensation. "Gortonnn...." She dragged out her Kings name in feared concern.

"Yes my love?"

"Run, run now."

"An odd time to joke do you not thi-"

"He will kill you, you fool!" She cursed, twisting towards him, her hair wafting across her face.

"My limits are broke, his body is wasted, why would I fear anything in this realm now that I am....I'm..." His speech was ended as he looked on is disbelief. Brekos began to glow, not his aura, but his physical being. His body began to blaze with light, cinders of white, blue and green spread across him. His snarl grew louder.

"This isn't possible." Lilith uttered.

Vixrol lay, looking up at a beacon of heaven, growing brighter by the second. He said nothing, he could not move, tears silently balled from him.

The dull groan shifted to a slight roar as the Angel bared his teeth, his gums bloody. In a critical outburst, the former Commander arched his back and tensed his arms, howling at the top of his lungs as his body raged with flames, removing any sign of his body. Huge shockwaves rocked the shores and split the earth. Rings of blurred energy erupted, fading as they expanded.

He had changed from a weak, shaking bird man into a billowing silhouette of flame. His eyes were replaced with flickering green lights.

"Damn..." Lilith ticked, shifting away from the danger, hiding behind the King.

"Very impressive display Brekos. Let us see whether you can use it effectively."

The shimmering being continued its scream before disappearing in an instant. Its only shadow was several dazzling embers. In a crushing swipe, the Angel clawed at Gorton, ripping his arm apart. The shining creatures rush created such force that the Demons body shredded away, continuing until his arm had completely dissolved.

Gorton was knocked back, terrified at the warriors Godly power. Unlike the previous battle, his arm did not regenerate, he was left with a spewing hole for a limb. He did not have enough time to register the pain, as he was hit with a barrage of pressure. He flipped and spun into the sea, plunging to its depths. Brekos turned his fiery eyes to Lilith, who for one of the Original Eight, was frightfully shaken. He tried the same approach again, swinging for the enemy with mind blowing speed. He failed, her agility saving her as she arched back, lying her upper body flat. His mistake was rapidly followed up by bone shattering knee to her back. A cry of pain escaped her, and similar to Wrath, she has never experienced pain on a high level before.

As she rocketed to the sky and broke through the clouds she was greeted by a flashing, bright abyss of stars. One in particular was large and prominent. It flared above her. Before she could react, she noticed what it truly was. A scolding hot palm seized her face and drove her down from the edge of the atmosphere. The couple smashed through the clouds once more, forcing them to part for hundreds of miles. Brekos pushed her through the toughened ocean, sending tsunamis in all directions. As they approached the ocean floor, he released her. Her face was branded with the outline of his hand. The intense heat evaporated the water, bubbling away insanely. With yet another merciless blow, she was tossed out of the sea, crashing into the side of the cliff and smashing through it, falling into an untidy heap, along with hundreds of bodies, members of both armies.

The surviving men fled, sprinting as fast as they could from the collapsing shore. Vixrol on the other hand, was helpless. The shockwaves from the clashes flung him around the land like a ragdoll. He was sprawled in the wreckage of the Commanders tent, snagged on a boulder.

Lilith on the other hand was already back on her feet, heaving, trying to bring breath back to her lungs. Her dress was in shreds, just covering her enough to keep herself decent. Her skin was torn and seeping, ocean water cascading from her body and hair. Regardless of rank, when an Angel reaches its last moments of life, no one is safe.

A tower of steam piled from the sea, leaping over to the land. Brekos stomped down in front of his target. Shining brighter than before. He raised his arm, ready to strike the finishing blow. Lilith summoned another inky cloud to her hand, as a final attempt at defence. In a quivering flash, her King blitzed to her aid, his remaining body leaping to the Angels rear. He pulled his bladed arm back, ready to thrust.

As the Angel sensed the Demons presence, he changed targets, focused on destroying at least one enemy. His arms whirled, trying to catch both devils with a critical shot. Clenched hands, he made contact. As he felt his knuckles touch his enemies, he popped into sight again, the flames vanishing. He was Human again, his blows totally useless against the two. He felt cold and numb. He looked down to his chest to see a long, black thorn puncturing it, and the tip of a bruised jagged arm poking through his stomach, breaching from his back.

It was over. He had done all he could and it still was not enough. He had failed himself, his men, and his God. He picked his head up and wobbled it to glance over the land. Disaster greeted him. Yet he smiled and chuckled to himself. "You are a good man." He whispered with his dying breath.

His body became limp as his legs gave out, his arms clapped against his thighs. The Demons pulled their blades from the dead soldier. The men who were still close by stood silently as the man who had lead them to war, lost his life. As the corpse fell to the ground, a faint green flash zoomed from its chest. It rippled across the battlefield, grabbing the attention of all those present. It danced across the landscape before giving off a dense glow before it faded. It seemed to cast highlights onto something. Everyones eyes struggled to focus, though the sun peeking over the horizon eased their strain.

Poised at the peak of a freshly made cliff, stood a tall, broad figure, the green fire dazzling faintly around it. The daybreak cast an enormous shadow of the man over the ground, stretching almost as far as the stricken, burnt man.

"Thank you Brekos, my friend." Congratulated the figure, its robe breezing around its legs, the sun emphasising the ripped tone of its muscles.

"Friend of yours? Take him!" Lilith obliged, kicking the corpse gently towards the man.

Gorton flopped to the ground, struggling to survive, his wings shielding him from the sunlight.

"Lilith...you put me through Hell, and now you forced this man to the edge of his humanity."

"I care not for your complaining, Human, now stand right there while I take off your head."

"Human?! Have you forgotten me sister?" Boomed the voice.

"Sister? What are you doing intervening with these affairs? Hmm...do you plan to be exiled as I am?"

The God paced down the cliff and across the scarred wasteland, to the side of his friend. His dark hair shimmered as he scooped up the body in his arms, his smashed collar completely healed since his fight with Hermes. "This battle is over Lilith, take your surviving and your 'King' home."

"And you shrink away with your mound of bodies, Wrath!" She smirked.

Wrath traced his footstep, catching sight of Vixrol, sprawled on the cloth. His heart sank as he glided over to the motionless soldier. "Forgive me Gabriella, I was too late to protect him from harm."

He landed by the mans' side. "Vixrol, it is time we left."

"I cannot, my body is broken."

"Luckily your Superior left you one final gift." The green light that he had recently soaked up transferred into Vixrols body, settling into him. "Brekos exhausted it of power, but the essence of it will be enough to restore your health." Wrath promised, as the soldiers rib cracked into place. Vixrol gripped the tent as his body crackled back to its former state. He was relieved that he could move. Once again his Commander had saved him.

Tucking Brekos under his arm, Wrath offered his hand to Vixrol, pulling him to his feet. Once they were prepared to leave, Wrath turned back to catch a glimpse of his fallen sister. She placed her hand upon Gortons back, then they blossomed into smoke, swirling until they faded from sight.

The armies retreated to their homes, both sides suffering heavy loss, but none more than the men of Hereteas. They had lost eleven of their Captains, thousands of men, and of course, their honoured

Commander. Despite all their loss, they had gained a
God.

# Chapter VIII
-
# A Friends Farewell

As Hereteas peered over the horizon, the sunlight grew thin, setting on the shuffling army. They were weak after their two day march, in desperate need of rest. The injuries and heavy hearts had caused the pace to slip to a near stop. As they slithered under the overhanging trees, chariots approached them, kicking splatters of mud at the returning soldiers as they passed. The drivers showed little if no interest in the mass of wounded men, much more focused on their responsibility of clearing the battlefield of the dead and returning them home. This was an act that they had grown far too efficient at.

Although the march was sloppy and unsynchronised, they maintained their formation, a forced habit after years of brutal military training. Walking at the head of the parade, stood two men as opposed to the usual individuality of the late Commander. Vixrol shared the same sinking feeling as his soldiers as he led them home, his eyes squinting to the grubby path beneath them. Wrath on the other hand, stood tall as usual, level with the new Commander, not wanting to take prominence over his position. His gaze carried to the city, noticing small, sprinting figures who poured from the gates. As the distance between the men and their home depleted, so did the quality of their organisation.

Strict, straight lines of soldiers became a sea of fumbling people.

The civilians who had left the protection of the city, women, children, came to claim their husbands and fathers and sons, plucking them from the crowd and swiftly escorting them back inside the walls. The mass quickly became a few. Even men with no family were assisted to safety, yet no one hurried to claim Brekos. His limp, scorched body was tucked in Wraths arms, being cradled like a mother would carry her child.

Before long the two warriors found themselves pacing alone, a fact that made Vixrol wince with heartbreak, wishing that his beloved had been there to welcome his return. Wrath noticed his comrades' hidden agony.

"Something troubles you Vixrol. It is unwise to lock away your thoughts."

The Commander took a deep breath as he strained to raise his head. "Before I met you in your prison, my fiancée and I found ourselves in a…well a dispute."

"Worry not, new friend, I already know." His look did not once shift to his friend, anticipating what his own return would bring.

Vixrol chuckled. "If I were a stronger man, I might have mustered the strength to question that, but for now, we will let it lie."

"You will soon be given a chance to test yourself, Vixrol, that is something I wish I could not promise. As for now, it would seem we must once again burden responsibility for this conflicts outcome."

A wave of red banners and armed men flooded the entrance to the city, trapping the two outside. They did not wish to cause any aggravation, so they hesitantly stopped. The centre of the gathering began to quiver and part, and the Royal Guard only moved for one reason.

"What heresy is this?!" Boom an angry, croaky man as he squeezed past the front line.

"My Lord." Vixrol bowed, placing a fist on his chest. "It pains me to say we have failed you once more. Lilith has tossed us to the pit of defeat yet again."

"Lilith?! So you have graced our enemies with a name now have you? And just who is this 'Lilith'?"

"Lilith would be my sister." Wrath intervened, swerving past the tense soldier.

"Well that clears this whole thing up then doesn't it!" His attention turned to the other man, golden robes clinging to his waist and folding to his shins. "I do not know how you are free and why you are here, but let me tell you tha-" His sentence was broken as his red mist settled enough for him to become aware of Wraths burden. "...Brekos...?" He whispered.

His eyes began to burn at the sight of the deceased man, hanging in his prisoners arms. "You..." He snarled, seizing the handle of his blade, strapped tightly to his hip. "You killed him you bastard!" In a furious swing,

100

the King drew his blade and drove it to the side of the Gods neck, his body spinning enough for his jewelled crown to tumble from his balding head. Wrath did not flinch, having nothing to fear from this man, all except one thing.

The blade was creaking against his flesh, shaking as the King forced more pressure against it, determined to behead his nuisance. Finally, the steel gave out, splintering and shattering into glistening orange shards as the sun greeted them.

The Kings failure was quickly backed by the guards drawing their own swords, a screech ringing in the air. As it died away, the group was in silence, Vixrol refusing to lift his head.

"I did not murder him, his death was of his own belief and judgement. Yes, he is dead because of the power I gave him but he acted through his own mind."

"That's a lie! Why else would you bring him here if not to boast of your kill?" He stepped towards Wrath to confront him, tossing the hilt to the dirt, looking up from his short stature.

"This is one battle where no blood was spilled by my hand. I bring this humans body home so that maybe, just maybe, you would grant a ceremony in his memory, one worthy of a solider and a man of his telling."

"So you're telling me, that Wrath, the Third of Eight, one of the most feared of Gods, was present in a battle and yet you brought harm to no one?" His attention shifted to Vixrol. "Are his words of truth Captain?"

Vixrols head bobbed in agreement.

"Commander..." Wrath corrected.

"What did you just say?" The King demanded.

"His title, it is no longer Captain. Before Brekos perished he appointed this man as his replacement, I expect you to honour his final instruction."

This King turned to re-enter his city, a guard returning his crown to him. "The task of assigning ranks falls to the King, not to members of my army." He contradicted, placing the gold upon his head.

For once Wraths eyes shot daggers at the lord. "My King that would be-"

"I am not your King!" He cried, spinning on the spot, this time his crown staying put.

"And I am no longer your captive!" His voice echoed with the same presence as a fully-fledged God. "You speak of your men as though they are the foundations of your empire, and yet here, now, you discard the last wishes of your Commander and friend! How do you see justice in this?"

"One of the other Captains is far better suited for the position and I will not be lectured by a sinner." Hissed the King.

"There are no others." Vixrol explained.

"No other what?"

"The Captains, they are all dead and gone."

"Why do you continue to poison my ears with lies?"

"I stand here holding one of the best men on this Earth, and you cannot even ask why he is not returning to you himself."

"You already explained this to me! He used your…" He flailed his hands, looking for an appropriate word to use. "…Curse, and for doing so was judged and dealt with as one of you, demonic filth."

Wraths grip tightened on the Angels body as he grew enraged by the Kings arrogance. "It is taking every ounce of will I have not to end you where you stand, King." The threat caused the armed few to joust forwards. "I will tell you this, and I expect you to listen. Brekos was forced to use the gifts I gave him, because your Captain, Gorton, drove him to it."

"We all make mistakes in battle, even Gorton. Regardless of his error I am sure he could have corrected it himself."

"Gorton is Liliths King now. He is nothing more than another spawn of Hell."

The King fell silent, a sense of threat seeped into his mind.

"In order for Brekos to stand a chance of victory, he ascended to a realm beyond that of man, and by doing so, became an Angel. Angels are essentially unstable Gods, unable to maintain a balance in their powers. They are similar to an explosion in that sense, devastating force which barely lasts long enough for a witness to comprehend it."

The King paused while he processed the information that he had been presented with, his head slightly dropped as he began to miss his deceased companion. "You may hold your ceremony. I will not be present." He said calmly, making his way through the company of men. He tapped one of them on their steel shoulder pad, engraved with swirling markings. "Escort these men to the Silent Chamber. There is no need to observe them after that."

And with that, the King vanished out of sight, followed by all but the one man he had selected. "Alright, please follow me." The soldier offered, his armour similar to that of the late Commander, before it was shattered by his first strike. Most of his face was hidden by the cheek guards of his helmet, long red hairs sprouting from its top.

As the three wondered through the streets, they became lined with civilians, creeping out from behind market stalls and stables. The path was quickly transformed into a mourning chain, bowing their heads and shedding an occasional tear as their loyal Commander sailed by. It was a horrifying contrast to what they had imagined, a returning hero bringing news that the war was over, greeting his people with open arms. No, instead of a proud victorious man, he was reduced to a soulless

104

body, tattered cloth drooping from his thighs, blistered stumps sticking from his back where his wings once hung.

The soldier guided them through the city to a large monument, an obelisk with a broken pair of stone, human feet, where a statue had once been placed. The guard halted and stepped to the side, turning to his right, revealing a dim, gloomy staircase, which led down under the structure. Vixrol entered first and was soon followed by the God. He had to slightly turn, just enough to fit inside without knocking Brekos against the walls.

They continued down the stairs until vision had all but faded. Vixrol stumbled slightly as the steps ended and a corridor began. "Where do you suspect this leads?" Vixrol questioned as the hallway grew wider with every step they took.

"I'm afraid I cannot be certain, yet I have a hunch." Wrath replied, slightly excited to see what would be waiting at the end.

The pair remained silent throughout the long, dark passage, the only source of light was Wraths glimmering yellow eyes. Tiny rays of sun broke through the darkness, highlighting the pristine craftsmanship of the brick work, symbols engraved into each one. As they turned around the final bend, Vixrol could not believe his eyes. They had entered an enormous temple, statues of an artist impression of each Original Eight lined the far wall. Three of these were smashed and crumbled, Wraths being one of them. He cringed slightly at the desecration of his image, along with the inaccuracy of the others.

He paced into the middle of the room where a stone plinth was extruding from the ground. He wandered across the marble floor, his sandals clicking in the silence. He lay Brekos down on the platform, straightening out the bodies' legs and crossing its arms over its chest.

"What is this place? How has no one stumbled upon it before?" Vixrol pondered as he gazed out across the landscape. The temple had been built into the side of a cliff, huge stone pillars supporting the tons of rock above it.

"As the King said, this is a chamber of silence. A place of secrets and wonder." Wrath informed as he too looked out across the lush green land, underlining the setting sun in a cloudless sky.

"But…what is it for?"

"Where else would a man be able to be alone with his thoughts in a time of war?" He tilted his head towards Vixrol.

The Commander met his eyes. "I suppose you're right. Wrath…I believe that I owe you an apology."

"If you are referring to our encounter back in the Chapel, let it rest. These past few days I have been through enough without trying to explain why I tossed the new Commander off a cliff." He chuckled, slightly smiling.

Vixrol laughed, sharing the joke. "Regardless, I misjudged you, had I known that the safety of man was and is still in your best interests, I would have never addressed you the way I did."

Suddenly he found himself dangling over a sheer drop with a rocky bottom, Wrath holding him by his scruff at arm's length. He began to panic. "Alright, alright I'll shut up!" He yelled as he squirmed. Just as quickly as he was in the air he was back on the ground, a few paces back from where he was originally stood. He let out a brief pant of relief.

"You should return to your quarters, I have no doubt that your fiancée needs to speak with you." Wrath ordered, still hypnotised by the scenery.

"That is if she can forgive me for what I put her through." He replied with a heavy heart, making his way towards the door.

"Have a little faith Vixrol, were it not for her, you would be dead."

"You'll have to explain that one Wrath, unlike you I'm not an all knowing being."

"Your Gabriella and I forged a pact, my freedom for your life. I swore an oath to return you to her alive. She will be waiting."

Vixrol smiled as he stepped into the mouth of the tunnel. "Brekos was right about you, you are a good man."

Wrath bit his tongue, tempted to challenge his title of 'man'. Though, he decided not to, and instead accepted it as a compliment from one comrade to another.

Vixrol left the room, leaving the God to enjoy the view. He stood for what seemed like hours, watching as his creation began to slip away from sight. For the first time since he was released, he had no reason to fight or rush, he could just absorb the moment. He finally turned his back on the picturesque scene and wondered across to the back wall, where he slumped onto a marble bench. He gave a little sigh of exhaustion and leant against the wall, resting his shoulder on the pillar next to it.

Day gradually turned into night before him, revealing a fresh blanket sky, littered with thousands more of his children. He smiled once again, feeling relaxed in the presence of nothing but himself and his creations. Moonlight created deep, procedural shadows as it clashed with the pillars. Brekos lay on the table, bathed in light.

Wrath tried to look at him and be happy for the departed, yet deep down, he felt as though another being had sacrificed himself in Wraths name, and for no benefit to be gained. His thoughts drifted to his past, and what he had been through and how different life was before the existence of demons and the war. He missed it.

A tapping shuffle broke the Gods daydream. He sat up slightly, seeing a small silhouetted man approach the table, upon which the Angel lay. As more moonlight flooded into the chamber, Wrath realised that the man was in fact the King.

He was surprised, when they had met earlier he was wrapped in royal purple robes with golden tassels swinging from its edges. Now however, he wore a silky white gown, with a deep crimson scarf around his shoulders, still decorated with tassels. There was no crown clinging to his scalp.

Wrath remained as quiet as possible as the King limped to the side of his former Commander, looking down at his scarred yet recognisable face. He placed his withered hand upon the corpses cheek, brushing it slightly with his thumb.

"Brekos Eastartes, my Commander and close, close friend, I pray of thee, watch over our people and our world. We face a threat greater than any of us believed." He let out a friendly chuckle as tears streamed down his wrinkled face. "And look at you…an Angel, knocking right on the gates of Heaven itself."

He turned and sat on the plinth beside his fallen friend, facing out to the wilderness. "When I met you as a boy I thought you would never become a soldier, you were so childish and provocative." He laughed quietly again. "Although from what the men tell me you haven't changed much, taunting Demons the way you did." He looked back down at Brekos, holding his crippled hand gently. "You had no family, no parents to take care of you and no siblings to care for. All you had was yourself. Yet when you ripped through your training and became a soldier, you were always a brother to your comrades. You never rejected any of them."

The King began to weep as he spoke to his friend, secretly wishing for a reply. "They looked to you in times of need, knowing you would do everything humanly possible to assist them. And then as you climbed up the ranks, you became more and more like a father. You went from being a starving, lonely orphan to having the biggest family in this land." Moonlight caught the tears as they fell, turning them into dancing shimmers of white. "When I became King you became a son to me, my one, true friend and hope."

The room fell back into silence as he wriggled in place to face the Angel properly. He raised his other hand and placed it against the mans' cheek. "Where are you now? Are you there? Can you see them? Is it all worth it, is any of this real?"

The corpse obviously could not answer his pleas. The King stood up and leant over the body, placing their foreheads together.

"I will find you again. Please do not be alone and do not be afraid. I will see you again." With his farewell said, he softly kissed the scorched brow of his friend and straightened his back, wiping the tears from his eyes, sniffling. He gazed down at the moonlit body, reluctant to let go of its hand.

"My King…" Wrath said softly.
The King was startled, he flinched as his head darted up and he gripped the hand harder.

"…It's alright." Wrath reassured, raising a hand, flat to his front to try and settle the old man.

"How long have you been here?" He sniffed.

"I never left, Sir." Wrath was overcome with sympathy and new found respect. He walked over to the table, standing opposite the King. "Even I had no idea how deeply you felt for him. Does anybody know?"

The King shook his head, burying his chin in his neck, a few more tears escaping. "No, no one knows not even he did."

"They deserve to know that he has stolen more than the heart of the people."

"No." He coughed, pulling himself together, still holding onto the body. "They would see me as weak and soft, in these times they need a solid leader."

"They just lost a solid leader, right now they need to know that the man leading them has a heart, and cares for his people and loves his people."

"I can care for my people without showing it, God." The King replied with false courage.

"Then why can't you release his hand?" Wrath asked, resting his palms on the table, flicking his eyes towards the Commander.

The King felt numb, frozen in defeat. He could not bring himself to let go, he wanted to always feel that he was close to his 'son'. He began to lose control of his sorrow again, silently crying, examining the face once again. He felt a firm pressure on his hand, his attention darted. Wraths hand was wrapped around both the Kings and the Angels, holding them tight. Their eyes met, tears streaming from one man, and sincerity spilling from the other.

"Letting go of his hand…does not mean you have to let him go."

The King began to bawl tears, shaking with upset.

"Hold onto this man, in your heart, there is no greater connection than that." Wrath hooked his fingers under the Kings, loosening them from the corpse. The King started to shake his head, unwilling to let go. "Don't let him go…" Wrath reminded, slowly peeling the fingers further.

In a deep breath of determination, the King closed his eyes, and relaxed to Wraths command. He felt his hand part with his friend. He tensed, fighting back tears, repeating the Gods words in his mind.

As clouds began to conceal the moon, the Chamber fell into near darkness. Forcing his eyes open, the King saw Wrath, stood smiling encouragingly over the table. "You truly wish to help my people?" He realised, parting his partial embrace with his company.

"My King, I was sent here to protect mankind from any evil it may be threatened by, protecting you has not only been my duty, but it has been my wish and desire." Wrath confessed.

"Then why? Why did you allow Atlantis to sink? All those people died because you did not help."

"And then you locked me away. I know not where this illusion has come from, this, false truth that I stood by and watched. There was only ever so much I could do to defend you, fending off both my damned brother and sister, I could have never succeeded."

"So…I was wrong? You had no reason to be bound?" The old man was shocked to learn the truth, that all these years he has been boiling with a lie.

"This is your land, you locked me away because it you considered it to be the right choice. I cannot fault you for that." He stood straight and headed for the exit, glancing back at the King. "But know that I am sorry for the lives I could not save and the pain my weakness caused. I promise you, even if it drives me to Hells doorstep, I will always push to protect your people."

And with another oath forged, he left, disappearing into the tunnel, leaving the King alone with his thoughts.

As Wrath emerged from the stairway, the city was dead, silent, not a single person to be seen. He made his way along the cobbled streets, glancing through windows and alleys, looking to see if anyone was there. His curiosity was left unrewarded. He started to notice a nagging voice in his mind. What if Lilith came back? Maybe the city was evacuated due to the threat. Streams of possibilities presented themselves.

He shrugged them off and focused on what needed to be done. He ventured to the Colosseum, the mud on the streets rolling away from his feet with every step he took, as though nature itself worshipped him. He carelessly strolled through the main gate to the battleground. It was still dark, he stood in the centre, creating a map in his head of how best to hold the ceremony, and also when would be best to hold it.

As the clouds rolled away, and the moon beamed down yet again, his attention was grabbed by the stands. They were full, every citizen of Hereteas was present and waiting patiently to say goodbye to the legend that had served them so well. Even the soldiers with life threatening injuries and aching feet were accounted for, wrapped in bandages and blankets. Some of them looked close to fainting, yet they waited.

Everyone looked weak and tired, frail after years of worry. This in itself gave Wrath the perfect idea for the ceremony. There were doubts in his mind however, he was unsure as to whether enough of his limitations had been lifted, so that he could perform it. Regardless, he knew he must try.

He headed for the gate, with the intention of fetching Brekos and beginning as soon as he could. However, he was cut off. Guards blocked all of the exits, making his only option flight, which is something he did not want to do, given the doleful situation. As he began to turn back to the stadium, the guards parted, exactly as they had earlier that day, causing his action to pause.

Through the partition, four soldiers delivered a large stone tablet, bearing the weight on their shoulders, and upon it, lay the Angel. To the heel of the men, came two more. It was the King, and by his side, Vixrol. Their heads were bowed as they walked past the God, through the small tunnel, and into sight of the crowd. As they entered, there was no applause or cheering, just the quiet hicks of crying.

Wrath followed behind the superiors. The soldiers placed Brekos in the middle of the sandy stage, still lying on the stone. Whereas the King and the new Commander paced up a set of dusty steps, situated to the edge of the desert-like ring. A hollow silence flooded the land as everyone sat and watched as the King took his position, Vixrol standing to his left, and Wrath, Wrath was alongside the late Angel.

"Citizens of Hereteas!" The King began, commencing the funeral. "We are here today, not with cheers in our lungs and joy in our hearts, but with pride in our souls and sorrow in our minds." He fumbled slightly, fighting back his own emotions. "We have been at war with Hell for many years now, and in that time we have lost many men. One of which, was Commander Brekos Eastartes. He was a brother to you all. He gave his life and suffered unimaginable agony just in the hope that he may free us from this darkness. But there are always secrets in the land of Kings, one of which is that not only was he a brother to you, but he was a son to me."

Wrath smiled at his feet as the King began to confess his true thoughts.

"He had no family, never did, and I was unable to find a bride in my youth and as such, we had very little to call our own. It pains me to say this, but the Eastartes bloodline has drawn its close. Many of you would no doubt wish to know why." The old Kings eyes wondered across to Wrath, allowing him to take his part in the terrible event.

"Brekos gave his life, defending this land! He has lived his life in a way that we can only dream of! He was an infinitely better man then you or I!" Wrath began. "He was once delivered to deaths door and, as a good man, he would not have suffered any upset because of it! However this land was not ready to part with him, and neither were those of you who needed him most! For this simple matter, I divided my soul with him, giving him new life and a second chance! Unfortunately, in his last battle, he was pushed to a place he had hoped he would never find! And yet, he did not turn, he did not run, he did not surrender, he fought on!"

The crowd struggled to control their weeps as Wrath lectured them, pacing around the body, looking up at all the dripping human eyes.

"When a God divides his soul, the recipient acts as a catalyst! The longer they remain united with the soul, the harder it becomes to control! Brekos was backed into a corner where he was given no other option but to use the gifts given to him, in one last attempt! Before he even began his ascension, he knew he could never again return to us! Once he engaged my soul with his body, he became an Angel, a Human God!"

116

Some of the crowd gasped at the truth, recalling the myths of the Angels and their nature.

"I wish not to mislead you! Despite his sacrifice, it was in vain! Our enemy is strong, and dangerous beyond any imagination! For a brief, shining moment, he was just as divine and formidable as any Demon! But we need more than that! We need to take his life as an example, and live by it!"

Wrath turned his head to the body, raising a hand out. Suddenly the tablet burst into prancing white flames, lifting Brekos from the ground. The stadium looked on in awe.

"He was a man! A man prepared to put his faith and hope in a God! In his memory I ask the same of you all!" He turned to the King and glared seriously with his shining eyes. "Resort your trust in me and allow me to fight by you once again! Let us bring Man and God together to defeat the Demons once and for all! Drive them back from whence they came!"

The flames became more furious, bleeding blue and green steam.

"My King! Will you allow this?" Wrath quizzed.

"…Lay the Commander to rest." He answered after a delay of thought.

Wrath grinned, knowing the underlying answer. "Brekos would not wish for any of you to suffer in his absence, and so he shall be your crutch in this war!"

With Wraths last promise, a beam of light erupted from the centre of Brekos's chest, crashing through the sky. A typhoon of wind whirled around the stands. Hair whipped and slashed, as robes danced and darted back and forth. The column of light grew more and more dense, shrieking with intensity. The sand from beneath them was sucked up into a swirling vacuum, thinning out as it began to spread. Suddenly it boomed out over with a low thunderous rumble. Turning into a glowing blue shockwave, the light tore past the witnesses. Some panicked, some were frozen in surprise.

Wrath remained confident, as did the King, placing his full trust in the God. The wave died away, the body was suspended in the air, upright, feet together and arms out to the sides. It faced Wrath though its head was hung, as if it was waiting. The crowd settled down as they noticed strange tingling sensations spreading through them. The wounded were healed, the crippled were renewed, the sick were cured. Using the last shred of the Commanders soul, the God had amplified it, and for once, carrying out the will of Brekos.

Wrath looked up to the hovering Angel and smiled with a true sense of happiness. "Go home, my brother." And with his permission granted, the Angel was transformed into shreds of light, zooming to the sky, up and out of sight, finally able to pass on.

For a moment, no one spoke, they did not even move. The King broke the silence.

"My people! Wrath…tomorrow we end this. Tomorrow, we claim our victory!"

For once, the crowd was unified in a cheer of rediscovered hope and pride in their land and their warriors. Knowing that when morning broke, for the first time, a God would truly come to the aid of man, entirely of his own accord.

# Chapter IX
-
# Prepare

The night was cool, chilling as the last stand of Hereteas quickly approached. The armoury was alive with crowds of confident soldiers, shackling themselves with weighty, silver armour. An occasional bellow of heat bloomed from the furnace. The thump and clang of hammer against glowing hot steel, threw sparks into the path of jogging men as they transported supplies to the chariots.

The busy mass of workers was overlooked by an already prepared King, his new Commander to his side.

"Do you think they are ready, my Lord?" Vixrol questioned, uneasy as the memories of their recent defeat haunted him.

The King took a moment to compose his response. He rested his hands upon the rotting wooden beam which lined the platform. "Our numbers are depleted, our resources are stretched, and above all else this is our only option. We have no choice but to be ready." A flare from the blacksmiths anvil presented a weaving map of creases across his regretful expression.

"It pains me to agree, sire. Although distraction is one luxury we cannot afford to allow ourselves." The Commander agreed.

The pair examined the workforce as they noticed it was disoriented among the organised rush. A middle-aged soldier sprinted up the creaky wooden staircase, hurrying to his superiors.

"My Lords." He bowed, awaiting permission to speak. Half of his head was shaved, replaced with a series of long, deep scars, stretching from his brow to the base of his skull.

"Speak Theros." Vixrol allowed, granting the King a few moments peace.

Theros straightened, his scruffy, fine hair wiggling in a brisk night breeze, seeping in through smashed windows. "Commander, the horses are ready and the tents are packed. The city guard have been alerted and armed, their patrol schedules are being discussed."

Vixrol paused while he sieved through various decisions and all of the outcomes they could create. A frightening knowledge that he was now responsible for the preparations for war, as well as its execution, crawled up his spine. "No..." He began to protest.

Theros was surprised by the Commanders rejection. The King raised his head, curious as to how Vixrol would handle his new, higher duties.

"Unpack the tents and saddle up another fleet. Call the guards from their posts and prepare them for battle."

"But...Commander?" The soldier stuttered.

"Trust me Theros, in this battle we will need every blade and arrow we can gather."

"And the civili-"

"Stop stalling." Vixrol shushed, taking advantage of his authority.

The soldier frowned in frustration, but remembered his rank. He quietly bowed and thumped back down the steps, fumbling through his comrades under the platform. With a screeching grind, he forced a reinforced door open and darted out to the city limits.

"Care to explain your decisions Commander?" The King questioned, silently summoning his warrior back to his side.

"It is as I said, we cannot afford to separate our forces."

"I know you are an intelligent man Vixrol, and I also know that you would not leave our people unprotected. What are you planning?"

Vixrol smiled as the King pressed the matter, never shunning an opportunity to demonstrate his sharp mind. "Our greatest asset in this battle is clearly Wrath. From what I understand, he has somehow regained a portion of his powers."

"But he shall be on the battlefield, what system can you possibly imagine where he can be in two places at once?"

Vixrol leant against the oak beam, similar to the King. "I have two systems where he can be of greater help. The first is one which I must still consult with Wrath about. If he could be capable of placing a shield around the city, it would obviously be well guarded."

"And the second?"

"From what my fiancée tells me, Wrath has the ability to see through the eyes of the innocent. Providing we place the innocent citizens near the gates, he can keep watch through them."

The King looked surprised but somewhat uplifted. "Vixrol..." He playfully slapped his Commanders back. "I did not know you were due to marry. Who's the lovely maiden?"

Vixrol fell speechless as he found himself cornered. He must somehow explain that he intended to marry a woman who was once considered a whore. He began to sweat with anxiety.

"Well? Spit it out man." Grinned the King.

"Gabriella." He spewed.

A brief pause seemed like hours, both relief and worry filling Vixrols mind.

"Gabriella? Your chamber maid?" He sounded frustrated and mildly insulted.

"Yes my King, my chamber maid is the 'lovely maiden'. However were it not for her we would still be trapped fighting for a stricken cause."

The King took a deep breath to settle his anger. "Explain." He ordered, massaging his brow with his finger and thumb.

Vixrol stood up and looked into the Kings eyes as he grabbed the courage to inform him of the truth. "Gabriella is the one responsible for Wrath being released. They both struck a bargain, his freedom for my safety." He gestured as he continued. "Speaking of which...she also told me what happened to the Chapel."

"Well I imagine that when he was freed he got a little...carried away."

"I wish that were the case sire. Unfortunately it may seem as though we face a new foe."

The King felt a shadow of horror engulf his body. He knew that Hereteas would struggle to defeat its current enemies. If they were faced with a new threat, they would be forced into submission. "What is this foe you speak of? In my city walls?!"

"It is Hermes, my Lord."

"Hermes? But he is our ally, he assisted in the imprisonment of Wrath. We were to supply the cell, he was the enforcement."

"A little odd that a he would be so eager to seal his own brother away, don't you think?" The King did not respond. "Well it would seem he is becoming his own, independent branch of Heaven. Although he hasn't broken any law, he has most certainly found a way to flex them. My worry is, how long is it until he takes that extra step?"

The men looked at each other, sharing one anothers fear and unease. The pace of the organisations began to drop as the men mumbled among themselves. The blacksmiths work ground to a complete stop.

"My King!" Addressed a man among the crowd, tucking his helmet under his arm.

"Speak man." The King allowed, still more concerned with Vixrols news.

"Well...some of the men have been talking, and none of us have seen the God since we left the funeral. When will he be joining us?" The room fell totally silent as they awaited a reply.

Turning to Vixrol, the King bowed his head. "Have you any idea where he could have gone?" He whispered. He had been so concerned with establishing his ranks, he failed to notice the absence of his greatest ally.

"Perhaps he is going through his own pre-battle rituals, just as we are?" Vixrol quietly pondered.

"A God who honours a war?" His eyes shifted up to meet his Commanders. They were greeted with a shrug. After a gentle sigh, he turned back to the questioning man and the cautious army. "Wrath is...equipping himself for battle, just as you are." He reassured.

"Perhaps if we could so much as meet him again, it could give us that boost we need." Another man requested.

The Kings mind raced to construct an excuse. Suddenly, the grand double door at the opposite end of the hall flew open. The wooden plains scraped against the stone floor, slipping to a halt as they reached 90 degree angle. The interruption was a welcome distraction to the superiors. The group of soldiers parted, creating a walkway along the centre of the building. A long shadow, surrounded by moonlight grew along the path.

"Gabriella?" The Commander queried loudly.

The maid wandered through the hallway, looking up at her fiancé. Slight gasps fluttered from the crowd, women usually forbidden from entering the armoury.

"What are you doing here?" He made his way to the top of the stairway, on his way to greet his partner.

"Stop there." She hissed, stopping her pace as she stepped out of the moon light and into the heat of the furnaces. Vixrol froze in shock as his lover was always controlled and compassionate, and never aggressive or mean. She turned her head to her lord. "My King..." She turned to her lover. "...Vixrol. I have given you your most valuable weapon and the last possible hope you have of survival. Now I ask for your debt to be settled."

"How dare you come here to blackmail me!" The King boom in disgust.

"Please!" Vixrol interrupted as he darted his attention, before composing himself, determined to handle the situation in a professional manner. "What is your request?"

"It is one that will no doubt appeal to your brutal nature. Before this war is done...I want Lilith dead. Not banished, not wounded. Dead."

The room was conflicted between roaring in agreement, and shivering in fright. Before either of the rulers could agree to her terms, booming echoes thundered around the hall. Heads turned to the entrance, it was bare, yet a broad shadow slithered under the archway. As the shade grew longer, Gabriella turned and made for the outdoors.

Before she could leave, a huge statue of gold and silver blocked the doorway, armour wrapped around its torso, spreading out over its limbs. A high metallic collar guarding its neck.

As Gabriella passed the statured figure, she turned her head. "And this time, make sure he comes to no sense of harm. Are we clear on this?"

"Absolutely." The character assured with calm resolve.

She quickly exited the room, her visit clearly one of aggravation and disappointment. Her spot was filled as the silhouette entered, taking long thunderous strides. The metal bands of armour spiralled down his legs, linking to a set of alloy boots, clinking with each pace. A final booming stride sank the armoury into silence, the humans looking towards the man in hair raising wonder.

"My brothers." The figure began. "At sunrise you shall leave this place, and it pains me to be honest but most of you will never gaze upon these gates again."

His words pierced through the ranks, inflicting fear upon them. Vixrol and the King did not mute his speech, as they too were aware that he spoke the truth.

"But before you ride, I urge you to ask yourselves, why do you willingly participate in this conflict?"

The silence was replaced with mumbles as men discussed their reasoning amongst themselves.

The moonlit man glanced around the room to personally address all those present. "Why do any of you follow your King into war?"

The murmurs grew louder.

"For those of you struggling to discover your answers, allow me to tell you why you are so blindly keen to engage in battle, with an enemy which greatly overpowers you."

The crowd hushed as the King leant forwards, eager to hear the conclusion.

"You ride to battle not for your King, not for your loved ones and not even for yourselves. You do not ride to please the Gods and you do not fight to save yourselves from Hell. The only reason you continue on is this…legacy." The glimmering symbol of armour stepped upon an anvil to overlook his audience. "You fight for tomorrow, you fight in the hope that once you are gone, someone will remember your name. Well my comrades, I promise you this. As Wrath, the Third Original, I swear to you that all of those who have given their lives to defend the future of this realm, and all of those who are still to be taken from us, their names will forever be remembered!"

His oath summoned an uplifting outcry from every man in the hall.

"And when those damned creatures peer over the horizon for our final stand, you will not fight alone!" Wrath threw a gleaming fist into the air, finding himself on an adrenaline high.

The building erupted into an empowered cheer, applauding the Gods words and also his dedication to his duty. Even the King joined in the celebration, pumping his fists as he once again felt a faint glimmer of hope for his empire. Vixrol however, was far less convinced. He recalled the battle between his own Commander and his new demonic enemy. Scenes from the duel flashed in his mind, a painful reminder that even if one of them was to ascend to the edge of godhood, it would still be insufficient.

Wrath turned to his Lord and glared with his pulsing yellow eyes, awaiting a verbal response of agreement. The King quietened and paused before he spoke. "Men!

Finalise the preparations! Your Commander, the God and I shall pay respects to the Prophets on your behalf."

The mass of soldiers continued their work with a burning new attitude. Both of the superiors turned away and wandered to a small doorway to the rear of the structure. As they journeyed out into the cool, fresh air, pacing down a stone stairway, their sense of comfort faded.

"Even with Wrath in our ranks, do you think we possess any chance of victory, Vixrol?" A slim sheet of fear coated his tongue.

"Despite how much I want to believe, I cannot. If you had been there my Lord, when Brekos fought with Lilith, you would share my vision."

Before they could discuss the matter further, a whistling soar distracted them. They halted and turned in curiosity. Contrast to the darkened sky, Wrath leaped over the armoury, only to slam down between the two. He slightly crouched on impact before quickly standing to his full, towering height.

"With all due respect my King, even with one hundred thousand men, the outcome of our struggle to come would be no different." Wrath warned regrettably.

"Tell me Wrath, why was Gabriella so cold just now?" Vixrol questioned, totally ignoring the current subject. The King shook his head in disbelief.

"My answer is entirely dependent on what you already know." He replied as the trio began to make way through a thin forest.

"To be basic, I know she set you free. I know Hermes ripped out her womb. Though I do not know how she is unharmed…"

Wraths eyes beamed down at him, surprised that he knew of his fiancées conflict. "Lailah." He whispered.

"What is Lailah?" The King interjected, becoming intrigued by the conversation.

"My King, even we Gods have aspects of ourselves and of our realm that we would rather leave unspoken. Yet I feel this information may soon become relevant to the cycle of this world." He sounded ashamed of the words he had spoken.

"Well, what is it? What is Lailah?" Vixrol pushed.

Wrath took a deep breath before he began. "At the dawn of the realms, eight Gods were born. These Gods are forever known as the Original Eight. There was a time when we did not interfere with your affairs, and instead continued to honour our calling. To ensure the functionality of the three realms. Heaven, Hell and Mortal. However, unknown to the rest of us, the Sixth had his own agenda. He was the first God to be judged by our King, the First. For the sins he committed he was condemned to Hell for eternity."

"You mean to say that Lilith is not our only concern." The King shuddered.

"She is but one of many. Nevertheless, despite sending the Sixth to Hell causing us greater inconvenience than otherwise ignoring him, the First also decided to send Lilith to the Underrealm some years later."

"And then they decided to try a different approach with your punishment?" The King suggested.

"Not as such, Lilith and I were judged for the same sin, and we were to be punished as such. Were it not for Tristens intervention, I would too be your enemy on this night."

The humans fell into silent thought, pondering over Wraths lecture.

"But…what law did you break?" Vixrol asked, looking up from the dirt.

"As far as the Gods are concerned…Lailah is the daughter of Lilith and myself."

The two jolted in astonishment, to even think that Wrath and Lilith could have been so close never occurred to them.

"But that doesn't explain Gabriellas attitude." Vixrol continued, gesturing with an open hand.

"Lailah is a second generation God, such a being is never supposed to exist. She too was sentenced, yet I had never known what her punishment was until a few days ago. As far as I can figure, Lailah is looking out for Gabriella, as well as the rest of us." Wrath turned to the Commander. "You have my 'daughter' to thank for your lovers survival." He closed.

Vixrol let a faint smile decorate his face, his hope now restored in the knowledge that they had both Wrath and Lailah looking out for them.

The group finally emerged from the woodland to be faced with a huge, pristine staircase. Waiting at its head, stood an enormous Cathedral, complex imagery engraved into its walls. To each of its four corners there were bold spires, reaching above its roof, a watchtower in the tip of each one.

The men began their climb, the King struggling up the many steps, his age bringing him down. Out of courtesy, the others slowed their pace, unwilling to let him fall behind. A royal red carpeted lined their footing, though dirt from their trek wiped into its fibres. Almost immediately, hunched, cloaked characters scurried in from the sides of the walkway, frantically sweeping and scrubbing at the rug.

With slight pants of exhaustion, the King reached the top, closely followed by his allies. They approached a high archway, leaning over the soldiers with carvings of warriors and demons lining its peak.

"Why does this place have no doors?" Wrath quizzed, his blazing eyes glancing over the artwork, slightly unsettled by the stories they told. They depicted men being slaughtered and eaten by twisted, ravenous creatures. Hardly the kind of reminder that warriors seek in a time of war.

"They claim it is to symbolise that their doors are always open. Personally I find it hard to believe that demons have never attempted to invade here, giving its lack of defences." Vixrol informed.

"Never?" Wrath asked in disbelief. Vixrol shook his head in response as the King hobbled, his breath finally returning to him. As they entered, Wrath felt an essence of dread creep under his skin. "And you say this is your holy ground?"

"Of course, when I was proclaimed a Prodigy I was trained here in the art of magic. I never was given a reason as to why they trained me though…" His own words unsettled him, never before wondering why of all the things he was taught, magic was his prominent subject.

"Ahh my King! Welcome, welcome!" Greeted a shrivelled old man, his hair wrapping round the back of his scalp, from ear to ear. He shuffled over and grabbed the Kings hand, doubling over and kissing it.

"Yes, yes my Priest." The King acknowledged. "We have come to seek your blessing for our armies' safety."

"Do not forget we need the location of Hells next passage." Vixrol reminded.

"Ahh my boy!" The Priest darted over to the Commander, also kissing his hand. "Come, come!" He insisted, waving his arm for them to follow. From the back, he looked like a heap of white and purple cloth, a trail of golden rope slithered behind him. "Am I to understand that this will be your final stand, my King?"

"It seems as such." He answered, wishing it wasn't so.

"Well not to worry, I have a gift for your Commander that could help favour the odds in this war."

Vixrols ears perked up, enthusiastic about any 'gift' he could receive from the Prophets. Wrath remained vigilant, uncertain as the dreaded sensation crept deeper into his mind.

The old, robed man hopped up onto a three-stepped platform. "Here we are." He announced, lifting a thick, stained, leather bound book from his desk. Lose pages displayed staggered corners amongst the crisp organisation of the novel. He grasped it in his hands as he turned, offering it out to Vixrol. The Commander, stepped forward to meet the offering, carefully wrapping his hands around it. "The Codex Magika." The Prophet entitled.

Vixrol examined the cover. A diagram of the stars embedded it, centred by decorative weavings of lined patterns. He smiled, knowing that the novel he now held contained the secrets to every spell and incantation the realm had ever known.

The Priest placed his hands on either side of the Commanders head, leaning forward and kissing his brow. "May the Gods bless you Commander." He moved over to the King, also blessing him. "May the Gods bless you my Lord." Finally, he found himself in front of Wrath, who was still looking the room over, nervous. "And what is your name my child?"

Wrath eventually bowed his head to make eye contact, his shining irises plunging the man into silence as he realised who was in his company. "I am Wrath, The Third Original." He introduced.

The shaking man stumbled back, his heel clipping the steps of his platform, knocking him slightly off balance, though he recovered. "Get out…" He hissed.

"Excuse me?" Wrath snarled. His company looked to their Priest, confused at his protest.

"You dare stain this sacred ground with your presence. Get out!" He cried, taking a step towards the armoured individual.

Wrath was not intimidated. He stepped forwards, slamming his foot to the ground, shattering the tiles under it. "If you wish me to leave, then tell me, who exactly were you asking to bless these men?"

The old man shushed, defeated by the Gods sharp mind.

"I do not trust you." Wrath muttered, squinting down at the man.

"Wrath please, he is a holy symbol of our people." The King pleaded.

There was a slight pause as the two starred each down. The Gods eyes narrowed further, yellow light slightly

breaking through his eyelids. "…You are blind to me."
He gasped, shooting his eyes open.

"Come on Wrath you should leave." Vixrol said,
agreeing with both of his elders.

"This man is not pure…If I cannot see through his eyes
then he has lost his innocence."

The pair of soldiers looked down to the old man, who
was growing shifty, fidgeting with the cuffs of his
robes.

Wraths nostrils started to flare, he winced in disgust.
"What is that foul stench?" He raised an arm to cover
his nose, slightly lifting his gaze from the man. Sudden
his head darted to the side, leering at the book the
Commander held in his arms. He stepped over, in front
of the King, seizing the book in his strong fingers and
slipping it from Vixrols grasp.

"Wrath what are you doing?!" Vixrol bellowed.

The God opened the book, flicking through several
pages. He lifted it to his face and sniffed it deeply.
After a moment, he flung his head to the side, coughing
before spitting on the floor, clearing his mouth. He
looked back to the Priest, his face still tight with the
remains of the smell. "Black magic…" He snarled,
slamming the book shut, tossing it back to the
Commander.

All three warriors stood over the man as he tripped to
the ground, breaking his fall with his forearm. His
attention shifted between them, terrified for his safety.

"I do not know what game you are playing here, but I can assume you were trying to condemn his soul by using the magic within this book."

The old man grinned in agreement, baring his brown, rotting teeth. He cried out in laughter before diving over the Kings head. The cloth around his shoulders flowed and warped as he landed on his hands and toes, like some kind of beast. He began to slobber, drool spilling into a puddle on the marble, tiled floor. He moaned and howled at his visitors, his eyes wide and insane.

Wrath held out his arm, stopping his comrades from venturing closer. He stepped before them to act as a shield. "It would seem as though your Prophet is little more than a twisted imp."

The 'imp' started to crawl slowly around the God, its teeth sharpening as its long tongue dangled from its mouth. Its eyes quickly shifted to the high ceiling, tempting Wraths eyes to follow.

"That's the problem Wrath…we don't just have one Prophet." Vixrol alerted, his head already tilted back.

Wrath reluctantly looked up. The walls and ceiling were alive with naked, creeping shapes, clambering over one another in unorganised chaos.

"I hate it when Demons play Man…" Wrath moaned.

A flicking echo bounced around the Cathedral as the dressed creature launched towards Wrath. He did not flinch. Instead, he planted his fist in the beasts stomach, with such force that cloth and flesh ripped from its back. It shrieked in agony, flailing and clawing at the God. He was hopelessly relaxed, still gazing up. Eventually he grew tired of the wailing animal, merged to his fist. He casually threw his arm to the side, sending the Priest flying into a thick stone pillar. A trail of blood splattered across the tiles, dripping from his armoured knuckles.

"Know any spells that suit this situation?" Wrath asked, allowing Vixrol to play his part.

"A few." He replied, looking back and forth across the ceiling.

"I suggest you take care of this. For me to use my powers in such a small area would put you both at risk."

Vixrol and the King were impressed, given that the Cathedral was the largest single building in all of Hereteas, even grander than the Colusseum.

The Commander, threw the book to the floor, clapped his hands, and quickly parting them. Faint flames danced around his palms. In sweeping motion, he whipped his arms to the opposite sides of his head, then jolting his right hand into the air, and his left to the ground.

The King stepped back in caution, unsure as to what Vixrol had planned.

Suddenly, the Commander launched his lower arm up, and his higher arm down. As the two passed, he scooped the flames into his left hand. As his arm extended, the embers exploded into a wild inferno, raging upwards. It flooded the top of the hall, scorching the enemies. Flames continued to bellow from his palm as crisp carcasses rained to the ground. Once the screeching stopped, as did the fire, flickering away.

The room was silent for a moment as Wrath looked to Vixrol, amazed with his powers. "I was led to believe that ice was your only power."

"There is a lot I can do that you do not know of." Vixrol grinned.

"We should leave this damned place." The King decided, making for the doorways with haste. He was furious that all these years he had been fooled. As the men followed, a high pitched whine struck the air. The three turned, Wrath driving his other fist as he spun. It crunched against an imps face, tossing it across the hall. It slipped to a stop as it crashed into a crowd of its own kind. Lanky, skinless demons closed in on the heroes.

"What is this? I just killed them all!" Vixrol cried.

"It would seem not." The King contradicted.

Wrath was confused by their survival, tackling his mind for an answer. Something caught his eye to the far wall of the Cathedral. Glittery black smoke waved up from behind the creatures. "The book."

"What about it?" Questioned the King.

"The book must be keeping them alive. You must destroy it."

"Me? What can I possibly do? You are a God, he is a Sage. I am but a man."

"No my lord you are a King." Wrath assured.

The King felt a sense of duty fall over him.

"Surely you wouldn't want to sit this one out." Vixrol winked, egging him on.

The King smiled as he decided. "Fine." He drew his sword. "Vixrol!" He addressed.

His Commander nodded, lifting his arm from his thigh to the sky, his hand open and fingers stretched. A whirl of air circled the Kings feet, carrying him rapidly across the sea of lashing beasts. He landed softly on the marble platform, near the desk, the book to the foot of its steps.

"How did you know he could do that?!" The God shouted over the grunting crowd.

"There's an awful lot you don't know!" He replied playfully.

Wrath shook his head and shrugged. "Unbelievable." He moaned, astonished at his lack of knowledge when it came to his own comrades. His complaint was cut short as the first of the imps attacked, leaping for the Gods throat. Wrath blocked its advance, cupping its skull before squeezing, caving it in.

Vixrol too found himself engaged in battle, swinging blades of ice through the throats of mutated demons. "Stab the book!" He cried, becoming overrun by their sheer numbers.

The King had made his way to the book, he drew his blade back, before lunging it into the dry pages of the closed novel. Nothing happened, the demons continued to regenerate and fight on.

"Stab it!" Wrath called.

"I just did!"

Wrath kicked a creature away, knocking back several of its brothers. "With what?"

"With my sword, what the hell else am I going to use?!"

"Well think of something else!" Vixrol encouraged.

Their argument was closed as the King looked up. A snarling animal looked at him hungrily, robed clinging to its arms. In a panic, the King pulled his blade from the book, launching the album into the air and onto the platform. He scurried away on his back, no time to climb to his feet. He lay across the steps as the beast prowled closer.

He swung his sword towards its face, though it was quickly knocked away by a powerful swipe. He was unarmed and helpless, his pride preventing him from calling for assistance.

The fleshless demon tucked its head back, suddenly pouncing to the rulers throat. Without thinking he reached back and grabbed the book, ramming it forwards and into the creatures mouth, wedging it open.

The beast backed off, shaking its head, trying to free its jaw. It pawed at its face like a mindless dog, struggling to breathe. The King smiled as he stood, pacing after the hindered enemy. As it shook wildly, it fixed its eyes once more on the King.

In one final blow, the King buried his fist in the animals chin, clamping its teeth through the book, piercing it. A maddening, unified scream filled the Cathedral as the demons bodies began to swell and burst, exploding into sparkling ash. As the fog cleared, the men found themselves alone, with the enemies, and the book, gone.

The trio looked to each other, panting after their battle. They quietly chuckled before erupting into full blown laughter. By human instinct alone, they had emerged victorious.

Though a phantom grew in Vixrols mind. Why was he betrayed? Was there any purpose to his teachings? Or was his entire existence built on a lie?

# Chapter X
-
# Welcome to Hell

"Hold on darling, we're almost home." She promised.

The mutilated torso did not reply as it descended down a dark, rocky tunnel. It was tied down, attached to a brittle sheet of dead bark. A pair of chains looped through its corners and continued up, shackled to the necks of two, lizard like creatures.

As they loomed from the jagged cave, squeezing under the stalactites, an eery red and purple light brought the grim wasteland to life.

The limp, dying body bounced on the mat as he was dragged over rubble and debris, his bride walking quickly by his side. He peered up with bloodshot, clouded eyes. He was surrounded by endless, black cliffs, riddled with a complex of holes and passageways. As he was dragged deeper into the pit, beady red eyes floated within the mouths of the tunnels, starring down at him. They would suddenly dart away, running back into the darkness, snapping with high barks and whimpers, before reappearing elsewhere.

Bursts of light from above caused his head to ache. He tried to focus his eyes, weak though he was, to try and catch a glimpse of the sky. To his horror, as his pupils shrank in the light, he knew he would never be gifted with a view of the sky again. Instead of clouds, there was ash. Instead of rain, there were bullets of glowing pebbles, spraying across the land. And, replacing the sky, wildfires blazed across, as far as the eye could see. He knew he could not return now, he knew he was in Hell.

The reptilian beasts, stripped of their skin, reared up and howled with demonic delight. As their large, clawed feet smashed to the ground, they darted in different directions, slipping the bark out from under their cargo, which tumbled to the ground.

As he lay, ash sticking to his dripping skin, he could finally see the bottom half of the world he had entered. Lava pits littered the landscape, toxic fumes bubbled from pools of dark, glowing oil. An array of creatures took interest in him, creeping around the twisted, root-like stones which encased the foot of the cliffs.

All of them were deformed, mutated. Most of them were built of exposed muscle, where others were like dry, mummified zombies.

"My King." Introduced a sweet voice, making his heart rate soar more so. His view was blocked as a bare silky knee, shreds of black dangling over it, touched to the ground. "I have returned from the Mortal realm."

"Hmm…and what concern is that of mine?" Grumbled a deep, sinister voice. It was out of the wounded mans' sight, and he was unable to move.

"Brother I must ask a deed of you. Please, heal this man for me."

"A man?!" It boomed, the sound of chains screeching as the owner of the voice climbed to his feet. A shadow rippled over the bride, her eyes closed, as though she knew what was to come. She began to make choking gags as her hands shot from the dirt, upwards. Her knees parted from the ground as she raised higher, her legs kicking and swinging as she was lifted into the air. "You dare bring a man into my realm, and expect me to save his life?!" His rage boomed with absolute disgust.

Lilith could not reply, faint whimpers creeping through her coughs.

"Answer me!" He demanded. A crunching snap rung in Gortons ears as he saw his Queens toes curl, droplets of blood parting the ash as they fell. "Hopeless bitch." The voice cursed as Lilith was tossed to the side. She rolled and bounced before slamming into a rock. Her face was spewing with blood, a deep gash across the bridge of her nose.

Suddenly, Gorton felt a tight clamp around his bladed arm. His body was dragged across the ground as he too was lifted. He could finally see the owner of the voice, the one who had beaten his lover. The first thing he noticed, were the mans eyes, blazing, furious red eye. They looked straight through the injured warrior. The 'Kings' skin was burnt and dry, slithers of lava peering through the cracks in his flesh. As for his build, it was broad and toned, possibly larger than Wraths own body. Embedded at the centre of his chest, shone a fiery red substance, carrying veins of magma across his body, fading as they climbed his neck. His hair was blacker than the stone which lined the canyon, it was pinned back, spiked naturally. Dim flickers of flame burst from the ground, casting light upon his face. He was a true vision of Hell.

"And you…you have the arrogance to take on the form of one of my own? And yet you are so weak!" The Demon insulted, swinging the corpse to the ground, kicking the ash away to reveal bare rock. Gorton hit the ground with a crash, shattering it on impact.

"Brother please!" Lilith begged, crawling toward them, holding out her hand. Her brother swiftly kicked it away with a dark, toned leg, detailed with blazing highlights. Broken chains, attached to his ankles, snaked into metal piles.

"I thought you had a better eye than this, Liltih! I once thought that you could never choose any worse than Brekos, yet here we are."

Gortons heart sank as his former comrades words were proved.

"What is your name?" The creature summoned, stomping over towards the limp, helpless man.

"Go…Gorto…" He struggled to so much as mumble, let alone give the reply that was required.

Suddenly, an intense pressure slammed into the mans ribs. "Answer Human!"

"Gorton!" He yelled, with all his might, panting in agony, too weak to cradle his stomach.

"Well well…perhaps there is some fight left in you."
He lifted his foot from the torso, and glared straight into
its eyes. "But know this, I am Saederol, King of this
realm. As such, I am the King of you…" He crouched
beside his new minion. "Though if you should ever try
to take my throne from me, you will experience a life
worse than this Hell." With his warning delivered, he
stood back up, ragged, torn cloth sheltering from his
waist to his knee. "Rebuild him!"

Tiny urchins scurried from the tunnels, slithering their
scarred, long fingers under Gorton. They dragged and
shoved him along the ground, guiding his body around
the side of the grand, rock throne.

"Welcome to Hell." Saederol greeted.

As Gortons bride and new King slipped out of sight, the
imps speed increased as they plummeted into a crater.

Yet again, he felt a hand grab him. This time its fingers
squeezed around his skull. All of the creatures that had
ferried him suddenly fled, diving into any cave
possible. Once again he found himself dangling above
the ground. His new handler was a tall, glutinous man,
its head minuscule, out of proportion with the rest of its
being.

The creature, its blubber clinging to its muscles,
moaned as it took slow, wobbling steps towards a pit of
sizzling lava. Gortons mind raced with fear, panicking
yet unable to show any evidence. The hairs on his head
curled and baked as he grew closer to the liquid inferno.
His skin blistered and peeled as he began to dip. Faint
cries of pain escaped as he was lowered by the brute.

148

The magma waved and climbed up his body, rising to his neck. Steam rose as the crackling of flesh filled the air with an unappealing odour. He began to bellow and scream in mind shattering agony. Quickly, the demon dropped him, plunging him into the pit, silencing him as the substance filled his lungs. The tip of his blade submerged, blocking the once great Captain from anyones gaze.

"Thank you, brother." Lilith honoured, her delicate hands wiping the blood from her chin.

"What further business do you have here?" Saederol questioned, slumping back into his throne, resting his elbow on its arm, and his cheek on his fist.

"The actions of the Mortal world seem to have grown...unpredictable." She informed, shifting herself up onto the rock which she had struck.

"Speak." He demanded, taking slight interest in the happenings above him.

"It is the Third, somehow he had been granted freedom."

"Wrath?!" He yelled in surprise, lifting his head from its relaxed slouch. "You mean to tell me that lowly brother of ours is still a pawn in this game?"

"It appears he is more than that. At first I could not recognise him. He was capable of flight, and above that, he wore robes, similar to those gifted in Heaven."

"So, the Gods have reclaimed him as one of their own."

Lilith shook her head, lapping the blood off her fingers with a sharp tongue. "No, he is still a mortal. From what I understand, his return must be approved by two Gods before he can once again rise to his godhood. It may be a misguided assumption, yet I believe he has gained the approval of at least one of our siblings."

"Hmm...I see..." The King fell into thought. "How will this affect the cycle of my realm?"

"Realistically, it probably will not cause much change. Although, just to be safe..." She stood from the boulder and gracefully tiptoed around her brother. "...Perhaps we should take him as our own."

"Demonise the Third? And what good would that deliver?" He argued.

"Well...I do not understand your quarrel. If we were to twist him into an ally, we would gain a great power, not to mention remove our greatest threat."

The fiery Demon arose from his seat, pacing forwards, past his sister. "In order for us to access the Mortal realm, Wrath must remain there. His presence acts as a bridge and without him, we would be trapped in here with an impossible chance of victory."

"Then open the Gate." Lilith persisted, diving in front of Saederol, placing a hand on his chest. "We have that power now, why not use it? If we permanently rip open this realm and the next, we will no longer need a 'bridge'."

"And this plan of yours, capturing our brother, how do you intend to carry out this act?"

Lilith giggled. "Oh my brother, you have been at your throne for so long that you have fallen out of sync with the worlds above. Are you familiar with the concept, 'berserk'?"

"Enlighten me." He grumbled, glancing down, the red in his eyes glowing a haunting shade of orange.

"When one of our family is sent to the Mortal world, to live as one of them, they lose almost all ties to their former selves. However, one thing the Gods cannot remove, is the will to win."

"Enough riddles." The King grew impatient.

"Simply put..." She heightened to the very tips of her feet, still much smaller than her ruler. "...If we were to back Wrath into a corner, and make him feel weak...he would lose control of himself. He would push beyond his allowed limits and by doing so he pollutes his very soul."

"And thus making him a Demon…" He looked up in realisation, his eyes widening as he grinned with sharp teeth.

"There is…one problem." She added, dropping to her heels and raising a finger.

Saederol grunted with aggravation, feeling misinformed.

"I have never seen Wrath in his berserk state, nor do I know what it is capable of. Alone I could easily push him to breaking point, but once he is beyond that, there is a very real risk of me being outmatched." Her voice hinted at controlled fear, genuinely afraid of her older brothers' Mortal potential.

"If need be, you can access your Paladin stage. Surely he has been restricted from that form?" The dark man granted.

"Use Paladin? Against him?! My final resort is reserved for a greater purpose than…Wrath!" She yelled, swinging her arm as if to cast something away. "No…I believe we have alternative means of ensuring my return."

Saederol smirked in agreement. "It always helps to have…" He swivelled his hand, slightly turning back to his throne. "…Friends in high places."

"I'm glad your mind is as wicked as my own. It is time for me to leave. I must prepare for our next assault." She began to stride up the slope which she had entered through, turning her head back before she left. "I will leave the arrangements in your capable hands."

Her brother sat back into his chair, grinning with delight as his mind created a grand image of bloodshed, and a dying realm as he claimed it for his own. Crunching a shard of blackened rock from the arm of his chair, with a powerful tug of his hand, he began to twiddle it between his dry fingers, plotting.

Lilith too smiled at her brother joy, despite his cruel nature, he was still her sibling. In a flashing prance of purple and black smoke, she flew through the tunnel, lighting it as she passed. She curved and spiralled along its complex system, blazing past a range of her deformed pets. They followed her trail loyally, chasing after her in mass numbers.

The Queen burst from the mouth of the cave, soaring into the ashy sky. Her cloudy presence swirled and thinned, revealing her usual form, hanging in the air. She looked down to the scarred plains which were her home, hundreds of creatures poured from the tunnels, quickly covering the ground with ever growing numbers. Their shapes ranged from flimsy, tiny goblins to strong, proud Demons, crushing the dry dirt with each of their steps.

Before long Lilith had amassed an army, greater than any she had previously ferried to the Mortal realm. Hundreds of thousands of dedicated subjects stared up at their Queen, mindless and ready to attack as soon as the word was given.

Lilith let out a laugh of satisfied excitement. Several strands of smoke spawned and began to circle her. One of them struck against her body, expanding and forming a dense panel of black armour, rimmed with silver details. More and more fog clashed against her, each one welding itself to her in a spreading sheet of metal. Eventually she was covered from neck to toe with the gothic wear. It was tight to her skin, emphasising her slender figure and lustrous charm.

Winged beast dived past her, filling the sky with their presence, swooping over the ground infantry. She looked on in proud awe as the army for her final attack, was complete.

# Chapter XI
-
# This is War

The scorching Sun drew sweat from the mens' brows, despite the sky being hidden by a slim blanket of cloud. Trotting boldly, the mortal army approached its destination. The blurred horizon told no tales of civilization or life, there was only sandy, brown rock, coated with whirling particles, as far as the eye could see. Dust carried on the wind, trying to invade the soldiers' lungs and eyes. Were it not for the cover of their God, ripping a corridor in the dirt to the head of the men, it would have succeeded.

The gravel and soil tumbled away in the path of the shining warrior, as though it were scared of him. The troops followed as their King and Commander rode closely behind Wrath.

"Wrath, how much further until we reach the battlefield?!" Vixrol asked, shouting over the howling wind. The God did not respond. "Wrath!" He cried again.

Suddenly Wrath brought his stallion to a halt, the rest of the army scrunching and shuffling to try and stop their own animals.

The King looked around, trying to peek through the thick sheet of blowing filth. "Well?!"

Again the divine being remained silent, his hair whipping randomly in the harsh gales. Finally, he raised his arm, bent, tucking his hand to his chest. He held his pose for a moment. His shoulders twisted slightly as his hand was pulled further back, restricted by his heavy armour. Suddenly, he lashed his arm out to the side, its speed creating a booming shock.

Almost in response to his actions, the wind vanished, the dust peeled away from the wasteland and towards the horizon, leaving behind a solid, clean slate. The world seemed a reddish shade of grey, even the sky had lost its usual vibrancy.

Every man looked around, examining the playing field, some letting the occasion get the better of them as they readied their spears, preparing for battle.

Wrath turned to the King and Commander with a grin of accomplishment across his face. "This is where we will end this war."

"Here? But there's nothing, what possible reason could there be for the Demons to come here?" Vixrol protested, gesturing with his hand before resting it on his thigh.

"It's simple, we are here. The Demons want this war to be over just as greatly as we do. Though our reasons are worlds apart."

"So if they were going to come to us, why have we spent half a day travelling away from my city?" The King asked, also unsatisfied with Wraths justification.

"Why ask a question when you yourself gave the answer? You said it yourself, there is nothing here."

"There was nothing twenty miles back from here." The King snarled, swinging his arm back to point to their tracks.

"I cannot blame your frustration, my Lord. For those who have never seen a battle between Gods, it is something they can never comprehend." His head dropped a little as his eyes darted to the ground, as though he were embarrassed.

"If you believe that you need such an area to fight, then that is your judgement. So long as you realise you'll be helping carry the wounded home." Vixrol joked, trying to ease the tension.

"As much as I wish to promise my services, I dare not." Wrath turned to face the commander, regret in his eyes. "This battle is just as much a threat to me as it is to you. There is no guarantee that I will be amongst those returning home." His reply darkened the mood further, overruling Vixrols attempt to lighten it.

A short pause ended conversation, as the three contemplated what disaster the death of a God would bring.

"So when will Lilith be arriving?" Questioned the King.

"That is something which I cannot answer, if they were here I would know. It seems as though we arrived early." Wrath analysed, standing on the stirrup of his saddle. He lifted a leg, intending to dismount. As his foot was free of the strap, he heard a dull ripping noise in the distance. It rumbled and tore across the terrain, bounding into view.

Wrath looked up, squinting as to see clearly. Rising from the ground and carving through it, were three huge, thick chains, bursting from below the surface. They continued to travel towards the army, climbing higher into the air.

"Oh, perhaps we're right on time." Wrath announced, slipping back onto his saddle.

Fiery clouds of ash bellowed from the head of the chains, tumbling and growing across the land. The smoke seemed to sprout thick, dense roots, weaving into a galloping structure. In unison, the clouds began to unfold, giving birth to three, gigantic hounds. They continued to dash across the desert, their muscles pumping with furious effort. Unlike most Demons, the triplets still possessed scraps of flesh. It clung to their bodies like loose, black sheets. Their eyes were empty, clear white spheres tucked into the front of their skulls. Acid splashed from their lips and their tongues bounced between their razor teeth.

"Well...that's not good..." Wrath shivered.

"What? What isn't good?" Vixrol armed himself as he questioned.

"As much as I do not wish to say this, my Lords..." He held his hand out towards the bounding beasts. "...The Hounds of Hell." He introduced.

"But they are but mindless beasts, surely you do not fear them." The King galloped forth slightly to rest by the Gods side.

"Oh by all means their existence does not faze me." He settled, slighting tilting his head to the King. Then he turned back to the creatures, stiffening his expression. "Yet I would be a fool not to fear their presence..."

"Well what does that mean?" Vixrol wondered aloud.

Wrath did not reply, instead, he jabbed the horses' ribs with his heels, commanding it to gallop. He rode around the front of the Commander, doubling back and trotting down the centre of the army. A narrow partition carved the force in two.

"Wrath! Where are you going!?" asked the Commander as he turned his steed.

The God turned his head back and grinned. "Run up!"

"Run up? What is he talking around?" The King discussed with his comrade.

"I honestly have no idea."

"Can that man ever give just a straight answer?"

"Perhaps if he were a man."

The pair looked at each other, the booming footsteps a constant reminder that they were at war.

"Well Vixrol, I suppose we should be thankful that he is more than that." The King turned his back, trotting to the head of his army. Soon, he was backed by the chime of fifty thousand blades being drawn.

To the rear of the mass, Wrath slowed slightly, enough to grab the reins of a horse, tipping the supplies from its back and guiding it away, following the trail they had created on their travels. He tucked down and fled full speed over a rocky slope. Moments later, he was out of sight.

At the other end of the field, the dogs jolted back, their back legs kicking forwards as they ran out of leash. They fumbled while trying to regain their stance. Once they were settled, their claws crunched into the dry, crumbling earth. They heaved, dragging themselves forward with relentless effort. As they prevailed in their attempt, stride after stride they struggled on.

A long, deep scar ripped along the ground, linked to the base of the chains. It shattered and gaped, splitting further, sections of cliff falling into its abyss. Suddenly, the back lip of the crack began to rise, pulling over the other ledge. It seemed naturally impossible for rock to fold in such a way, yet, nothing in the Mortal realm required reason for it to be.

It rolled across the sky, like a tidal wave of rubble and dirt, unveiling a deep, shadowed passage way.

"I agree with Wrath, this is not good…" The King decided, struggling to calm his shuffling stallion.

Dark fog began to pour from the gate, spilling over the land, some rising to the air and blocking out what little sky was available. The world sank into a grim, dark blue shade, as though a thunderstorm would erupt at any moment.

With a crashing roar, the ground stilled. The hellish canines had succeeded in their mission, and now were able to fixate their marble eyes on the men, gathered in the distance. They jerked at their leashes, desperate to break free, just as any dog would if it detected an intruder. They yapped and howled, spitting drool wildly as they squirmed. Their bark had such volume, such force that it caused the mens' chest to quiver.

Shrieking, a high pitched whistle strung from within the darkness, calming the beasts immediately. From the black, walked a single, dainty figure, pinging with each step onto the toughened battlefield. The shape was simply too far away to distinguish an identity, yet Vixrol had a strong idea of who it could be.

"Lilith…" He snarled, twirling his blade around his hand.

"You can see her?" His Lord inquired.

"I do not need to see her face to know it is her. The stinging in my spine is clear enough."

The single silhouette at the far edge of the plain, ended her advance. She held her hand to the sky, generating a folding, dark cloud in her palm. As her fingers wrapped around it, it ripped into her usual, long black spear, the tip of which aimed towards the Sun.

Liliths arm dropped until her weapon pointed at her enemy. In response, the black well sprung into life, skinless humanoid beasts raced from its shade. They bounded past their Queen, closing down on their Human opponents. The final crusade had begun.

# Chapter XII

-

# Long Awaited Revenge

"My brothers!" Vixrol grabbed the attention of his subordinates as he dashed across their frontline. "This is the day we have been waiting for! This day, will be our final stand, the last stand for mankind and all its promises!" He turned to gallop the opposite way. "Do not be afraid! Do not mourn for those who fall, because they do so with hope in their hearts, the hope that one day, their actions will be reflected upon our world!" Finally he took his place by the Kings side, slipping his helmet onto his head, a long, narrow point covering his nose. "We are Heretians! Warriors amongst men! I cannot think of a better army to bare the weight of this realm!"

The enemy forces rushed towards them, just close enough to differentiate one creature from another. Their muscular claws, pawed at the ground as they advanced on all fours, each one kicking a storm of grit.

"Hereteas!" The King joined. "For tomorrow!" He cried, lunging his blade forward as he whipped the reins against his armoured steed. His words were followed by a ground shaking roar, his entire empire crying out in passion as they began to ride, sailing towards their enemies.

Their bellows continued as the two divisions closed down on the Demons. The battlefield was alive with roars and howls and the time for the first strike grew closer.

Vixrol planned ahead, quickly constructing a surprise attack. He whipped his armed hand out to the side, loosening his index and middle finger from the grip. Dim flickers of light sparked to the wing of the field. Furiously, he swiped his arm back across his chest, coursing the flare between the conflicting realms. The air exploded into a high, raging wall of flames, cutting one army off from the other, yet they both continued.

As the Commander readied a small vortex of wind around his weapon, a thunderous boom shuddered across the wasteland. Instantly following, a gleaming blur blitzed between the King and Vixrol. To the side of the army, two shining bursts, one to each side, raced level with their blurred companion.

Concurrently, the three ripped through the fires, directly confronted by a sea of red and crimson creatures. The bright objects were the first to make contact, gleaming hugely as they did so. In identical whines, they erupted into soaring pillars of white smoke, just as Wraths first steed had against Hermes. The power of the explosion ripped hundreds of nearby beast apart, shredding the muscles from bone, before they too were smashed.

The figure to the centre froze to a stop as the flames folded away from it. With buckling accuracy, it wedged a fist through the skull of a nearby Demon. The shock of the impact burst its head, with yet another hundred of its allies suffering the same fatal pressure. Panels from the attacking arm twisted and bent as they flew from the body. Blood showered upwards in a rippling display, the frontlines of the enemy totally annihilated.

The soldier was hovering, staring at his naked arm as bodies collapsed around him. "Petty Mortal armour." He snarled.

His groan was shattered as one of the larger Demons made its presence known, bellowing with an animalistic growl, its jaw stretching down to its chest. It too had blank eyes, slightly decorated by scribbled veins.

Wrath touched to the ground, settling in a mid-sprint position. Pulling his arms back, he launched forwards, head on into the oncoming assault. He ripped through beast after beast, swinging and twirling, catching them with devastating blows.

The cheer of men was once again uplifted as they finally made contact. A heart shaking thud rumbled as the strong chests of stallions, battered against bare muscle. Their conflict was far less elegant. Men were stolen from their horses as Demons pounced upon them. Others were slaughtered by as little as a passing claw. Regardless, they did not retreat. They continued to jab and slice at the enemy, taking a greater number than they lost.

Waves of razor sharp wind spread into the mass, as Vixrol infused magic into each of his strikes. Moments into the battle and the plain was littered with dismembered bodies and spraying blood.

Despite the Kings age, he pushed with as much effort as every other man. His long, silver sabre, jousting and gashing into his enemies, the beings which had caused him Hell on Earth.

In the midst of the chaos, Wrath approached his target. It was enormous, a warped, towering creature. It was uneven, one of its arms substantially heavier than the other, lined with muscle, whereas the other, was built of brimstone. Slim streaks of steaming lava crept through the gaps. Catching a glimpse of the battling God, the Demon raised its rough rocky arm towards the sky, preparing to attack.

This did not go unnoticed. Picking up his pace, Wrath knew he must hurry, if its arm were to shatter, his allies would be devoured by an ocean of liquid fire. Finally he had fought his way through to the base of the titan. He crouched and yelled, gradually getting louder. The rim of his armour and silhouette became lined with white and blue highlights. In a burst of speed, immeasurable by man, he rocketed to the sky, driving through the base of his enemies' chin before breaking through its skull with a bone shattering crunch. A trail of glittered light lined his path, quickly fading as his speed dropped after his technique.

He twisted in the air, casting the blood from his arm and he looked back at his victim. The plates of dripping steel shed from his other arm and a section of his shin. "This is ridiculous." He cursed as he watched the panels clang to the dirt.

The giant froze as shards of its skull continued to tear. Crashing to the ground, its knees fell. Its' lava filled arm slowly descended towards the battle. The God gasped as his heart pounded with fear of losing his comrades. Before he could react, his target was swept away by a breeze, burning it into ash. Though the wind was not strong enough. It fell against the rock, spreading into a plume of black fibres. To Wraths wonder, the Demons death had resulted in its instant cremation, a conclusion which he would not take for granted.

As the last of Hells forces exited the Gate, the battlefield was overrun, fighting characters stretching for miles. Fate had not favoured the Human cause. Each of the surviving men had been circled, many of them losing their transport as they were funnelled into tight groups across the land. Vixrol stuck close to the King, maintaining his sworn oath.

"Vixrol! Think of something!" The King cried in a state of panic as he lashed wildly at the brutes.

"That would not be so much a challenge if I wasn't fighting for my life, sir!" He too was engaged in combat.

"Well then hurry it up!"

The Commander continued to defend the men to his flank while his distracted mind burned, trying to create a solution. His eyes were momentarily drawn to the sky as dull flickers of lightning peeped through. He grinned with inspiration.

Reaching back, he cupped the side of a soldiers neck. "Protect that King with your life, brother!"

The warrior did not protest or even hesitate as he rapidly jumped forwards to take Vixrols place. The Commander pushed his way through, struggling into the centre, to the back of the fumbling men. When he reached it, he held his bloody sword to the sky, the men around him backed off, knowing what he was now capable of.

Another sheet of lightning twinkled, followed by flash after flash. Digging the tip of a spear into the dirt, Vixrol carved a circle, no bigger than his hand. The sky roared again. Spinning the tip of his blade down over, he knelt, stabbing it deep into the rock, to the centre of his carving. The light from above pierced the cloud, striking the hilt of his blade and running straight into the ground below. The tingling shock spread outwards, creating a ring of bright blue bolts around his allies.

Instantaneously the dirt outside the line came to life, exploding with long, twisted spires of glass, at least twenty layers thick. The clear spines penetrated the Demons and either ripped away limbs, or ended them where they stood. The glass acted as a shield, completely covering them from the riots on the ground, however they were open to aerial assault.

Gargoyles and wraiths swooped above them, hurling spears and flames at the trapped group. Without looking up from the ground, Vixrol let out a howl of strain as he forced his blade to twist. It suddenly gave out to his will and carved a hole into the bloody rock.

The core of the pointed towers danced as electricity pulsed up their length. In a blinding flash, the tips released an almighty strike, shocking the creatures in the sky and throwing them to the bloodbath. A pounding clap accompanied the display, booming across the air.

The crowd shuffled as Vixrol drew his blade from the crater, the King weaving his way through. The pair looked at each other and smiled. "You cannot deny that was your greatest spell yet."

"Actually, my Lord, that was mostly science."

The Kings smile enlarged. "Well then, use your science to get us out of here."

Vixrols grin vanished as he looked around the men, a blank expression across his handsome, spattered face.

"You do know how to get out of here…Commander?"

"Erm…yes?" He answered, not convinced with his plan. Though, this was battle, there is no time to hesitate. So without a moments' notice, he whipped his empty hand into the air, launching his comrades and himself up and over the obstacles. Small cyclones surrounded their feet to carry them to safety. Despite this, everyone flailed in unsteady waves as they felt their stomachs rise in their chests.

The landing was somewhat cushioned by unsuspecting creatures, as the blades of men jabbed into their backs and necks.

This caught Wraths eye, sending him straight into hysterical laughter as he hovered above the anarchy.

The image of falling, wiggling men repeated in his mind.

"I'm glad to see you are finding this as entertaining as I, brother." Taunted a toughened, feminine voice, silencing his amusement.

Wraths shoulders fell, his fists tightening as he slowly turned to greet his visitor. "Lilith...I had hoped to test my new limitations a little further before meeting you in battle yet again."

"Oh please brother, do not fool yourself. It is direly unattractive." The Demon whispered, pacing on the air and running a finger along her brothers' grubby chest plate. "I can see it in your eyes that you live for this, the act of war."

"You think I live for this? This...mass sin?"

"Magnificent isn't it." She said, looking down to the disaster below, scraping her fingernail away from the metal. "How the mere threat of death can bring forth such desperate resolve."

"Do you feel nothing from this?" Wrath asked, turning to his sister who had wandered past him. "Are those not your children down there, dying?"

"As though I could be so heartless, of course watching this hurts. Yet I love it." She grinned with evil intent in her eyes.

"Well...if you love this so deeply perhaps I shall give your heart reason to break..." Wrath threatened, pulling the last of the armour from his right hand.

"Your words are but empty promises Wrath." Lilith turned and shunned her opponent.

"You commenced this battle with a critical mistake. Never should the Hounds be present in my wake. In opening the Gate you have sealed your own demise."

"You intend to slaughter my pets?"

"Your mind is sharp sister." He grinned, preparing to approach his next target.

"You overestimate your potential, Third."

"And you cannot comprehend the rage that false punishment breeds in ones soul." As his final warning was given, he rocketed across the scene, sweeping down towards a shedding gatekeeper. Lilith made no attempt to follow, instead watching with her metal arms folded.

Drawing his hand back, his palm burst into white and green flame. He raised his left arm, using it as a guide for the attack he was about to unleash. Finally he was within striking range. He roared as his arms tensed, strands of hair streaking across his brow.

"Being of Hell...burn!" He cried, throwing his shining hand forth. A cannon of light engulfed the centre canine, so dense that the earth itself began to quiver. Energy spread to such a scale, that even the Gods closest comrades took a moment to gift themselves a glance. The cone of power blazed into the gate, crashing around the victim. As his howl faded, so did his attack.

The dog was out of sight, consumed in an ocean of mixing white and black smoke.

"May your sins be vanquished along with your soul." He muttered, bowing his head at the site of his historic victory. Suddenly, a deep groan unsettled the God, summoning his head upright once again.

As the smoke cleared, a set of clouded white eyes stared to their attacker. Wrath stiffened with terror. Despite using one of his greatest abilities, at point blank range, the enemy was entirely unharmed. In a cracking whip, the Hounds barbed tail launched him away, his determination shattered as he drifted further from the gate. He steadied to a halt.

"My my, how embarrassing for you." Lilith teased, covering her lips with the tips of her fingers, sliding down to Wraths level. "I tried to warn you but you just won't listen."

"You're pet...that...fucking beast...how did it withstand the anger of a God?" His head was tucked into his chest as his clenched left hand crushed the armour around it.

"You are not a God Wrath...it would be wise for you to adjust to that truth." Her voice suggested a hint of sympathy, as though she could relate to his torment.

"When did I become so weak..." He snarled. Air pulsed in short violent bursts around him. His head shot up. "This is your fault...you have put me through Hell..." His sharp yellow eyes deepened, though they become polluted. A thin red mist spread from his shrinking pupils.

"You know nothing of Hell!" Lilith argued, crossing her arms over before flinging them out to the side, the black alloy on her wrists grinding.

"Enlighten me..." Again, he snarled.

Lilith chuckled. "You sound exactly like the Sixth."

The crimson ripples in his eyes spread, equally dividing it between red and yellow. He bawled with bottomless rage, his cry echoing as he pulled his arm back. In frantic impulse, he slammed his hand into Liliths face, clasping it with his muscular fingers. His actions sent the couple hurtling back to the battlefield, Liliths body dragging down as her head was forced through the rock.

Stone billowed in rising waves as the Demon Queen was pushed further into its depths. The kicking rubble tossed creatures through the air, shattering their spines as they returned to the ground.

At the bottom of the crater, Wrath continued his grip, covering his sisters' eyes. "It is unwise to push me, Lilith."

"Well...let us see how far you can be pushed." As she established her new task, she slapped the Third with the back of her hand, freeing her head and launching him from the canyon. He tensed his stomach during his

173

ascent, driving his hips to twist, regaining control of his flight and jolting to a stop.

Three slim gashes opened on his cheek, blood trickling along his jaw. He lay amongst the clouds, starring at the sky, baring his teeth in building anger. His entire body tightened as he grew tired of being helpless against his sister. His irises became closer to being completely transformed.

A faint soaring pitch rang in his ears. He knew his enemy approached. Suddenly his head began to burn, his mind quaking and twisting into a primeval form of itself. Cupping his head he forced his focus back to the battle. The whistling howl was upon him.

Parting his hand from his face, he thumped his fist to his side, spinning into his rival. His knuckles bounced against her cheek, returning her along the path she had flown. With her ambush a failure, Lilith was unable to defend against Wraths own assault.

Her plummet was broken as a bone shattering knee crashed into her back. She whimpered as the air was knocked out of her, black locks of hair springing in the rebound. Shards of her charcoal armour burst from her stomach, revealing her smooth, tanned complexion. Her eyes widened to find an enraged God floating beside her, one leg raised to her spine.

As he lowered his leg, the crippled Demon swirled upright, clutching her back. She struggle to straighten, but was instantly forced to crease as her muscles tightened and ached. As her brother took a booming step towards her, she retreated several meters.

Casting her hand behind her head, she summoned her weapon of choice. She screamed, throwing her spear directly towards her brothers' heart. The air around him throbbed yet again, disintegrating the shard into a waving cloud of black powder.

Lilith backed away, her fear spreading through her body as she realised she had driven the Third to a place he had never before reached. Her plan to demonize him was succeeding, yet she was alone, nothing more than a quivering woman before a storm.

His usual golden eyes had thinned into slim halos of light. Lilith could not look away from them as he paced closer, steam flourishing from every step.

"Wrath, wait. Let us stop this for a moment. I know that you would not want to kill me as one of my own. Calm your anger and do this as the God you are."

"Calm my anger?" Wrath started, glaring into his opponents eyes. "Your actions stripped me of my godhood..." He ripped a panel from his chest. "...Confined me to years of imprisonment." He tossed his right shoulder pad to the wayside. "And you ask me to abandon my hatred for you?! No...were it not for hate, my mind would have broken long ago." The air warped yet again, blowing plates from his less defended side.

Lilith shuddered with terror that was all too real.

"There is a young woman, back at the city, who demands that you be killed before this day is through.

And I intend to carry out her wishes as such. As a God..." Segments bellowed from his left leg, revealing a bulky, toned thigh. "...Or as a Demon." He stood before his sister, their gaze locked. "I will end you."

Lilith gasped with fright as her brother words oozed with promise. She pulled herself upright and formed another spear. In response to her preparation, Wrath raised his right foot, kicking it towards her bare stomach.

She placed the pole across her body, gripping it in both hands, in an attempt to block the attack. It failed. The glistening steel boot of the God cleaved through the staff and buried into the Demons torso. The force of the strike, alongside the expansion of the dense, shattered matter, was enough to banish Lilith from the sky. Clouds completely vanished as they folded away.

Vixrol looked up as he heard the clash. A black trailing mass blistered towards him. He quickly leapt to the side, the mass just clearing his arm. The impact threw him to the air, along with tens of other men and creatures.

The God looked on, preparing himself for what would be the final strike. He grinned as madness crept in, becoming drunk on his own power. His blades of hair stiffened as he stared insanely. Bands of light blessed his figure, running along the edges of his remaining armour. His power possessed a darker nature than it had previously, flickers of white and blue were accompanied by glimmers of red. With a ferocious flash, he dived towards the ground.

Tipping a triangular boulder away, Lilith sat upright in her crater, confronted by a shining light, blistering through layers of smoke and air.

"Wrath no!" Vixrol pleaded, too close to the target to have any chance of escape.

Wrath continued with total disregard for the lives of the innocent, centred on murdering his fallen sibling. The distance between the two greater beings rapidly shortened. Lilith could not move, Wrath was focused. He flooded with superiority, a sense of undeniable position, greater than he had ever felt. Moments away from contact, his heart claimed victory.

Suddenly, the charged God halted, a crushing force catching him across the chin. His head tilted back as his body seemed to wheel slowly in the air. A crescent of debris and dust retreated sharply as it climbed into the air. Wrath was once again hammered, this time the pain spread from his abdomen. He was stationary above the ground as he doubled over. A third strike, finally to his face, pinned him to the ground. He lay disorientated. Though his eyes were clamped shut, he felt as though the world still raced by with extreme pace.

"Y....You...?" Vixrol uttered, slightly relieved that Wrath was unsuccessful.

"It's about damn time! I almost died!" Lilith screamed, a knot in her throat.

"If you wish to pin the blame, accuse the Sixth. I came as soon as I was notified."

The voice was familiar to the Third. He struggled to open his eyes, yet the incredible shift in velocity left his body to recover. A creaking object settled onto Wrath throat, slightly cutting away his breath.

"Perhaps I can finally lay this feeble oath to rest, brother."

The God finally had enough, he must open his eyes, desperate to prove that his ears were lying. Focusing his strength, his mainly red eyes peered open. To his horror, they told the same tale as his memory. Standing above him, a foot against his throat, stood Hermes, looking down at him, as though he were just some hunted kill.

The Fourth had joined the fray, also committed to classing this as the absolute final battle.

# Chapter XIII

-

# White Eyes, Black Soul

In the presence of a true God, the demonic foot soldiers lost their keen lust for killing. They cautiously crawled away, trying to flatten themselves against the soil. The huge, elite Demons however, though superior in strength, they lacked intelligence.

Bounding forth on four of its six legs, a ravenous titan threw its fist down towards the glowing God. With a grin, Hermes vanished, leaving the Third in the path of the approaching fist. It made contact. Wrath was forced, crunching through layers of brittle rock. Gashes in the ground spewed dust and dirt as they circled the impact.

He cried out in pain, gripping at the two furthest knuckles. His legs squirmed as he could feel his lungs starting to collapse. The scream dwindled in to a breathless whine as his face tightened.

"Is this it? This is what I came for?" Hermes mocked, walking to his sisters side. "To think you were struggling against this lowly Human."

"Or perhaps your introduction has left him a little delicate." Lilith defended, crackles of spitting earth accompanied her words as Wrath was forced deeper.

Hermes paced to the edge of the jagged crater, looking down at his writhing sibling. "I disagree. From what I have seen of him here today, I think he has just grown weak. Too close to mankind to remember who he is and what he should be capable of."

"Enough..." Decided a wheezing voice to the bottom of the indentation.

"Enough? Of what? Of being a doll for us to play with if we find ourselves in need of entertainment." Lilith joined Hermes by the edge, shadowed by the enormous arm.

"Enough..." His whisper became a snarl.

"No, perhaps he has grown tired of trying." Lilith turned her head down to the trapped God. "Trying to save this world from our inevitable rule. Trying to repent for his sins...Trying to prevent another massacre like Atlantis."

Wraths eyes snapped open as his teeth began to grind. "I've had enough!" Clawing his fingertips into the fist, Wrath drilled pressure up through the skinless arm, shredding it as strands of muscle tissue released and whipped. As the fleshy ropes tore through the air, they faded into snakes of ash. Soon the entire brute was fading away and blowing on the wind.

"I have had enough..." He rolled, pounding his knuckles into the already crumpled dirt. "...Of this war." He pressed himself up to his knees. "I am tired of always fighting for the protection of this world." Stumbling to his feet, he stared at his sibling, the yellow in his eyes all but gone. "Just this once, I will not fight on behalf of the living beings of this realm. Nor shall I give you bastards the satisfaction of looking down on me. Hermes...Lilith. You should not have come here on this day."

"Well I agree, coming here was a waste of my time. If I wanted to see a wobbling excuse for a creature, I could have gone to the ocean. I am positive that there are more than enough sailing bodies at its floor."

The air around the Third rumbled, its distortion stronger. "You know not what your actions cause."

"On the contrary. Lilith and I know exactly what our actions will bring."

Wrath looked up, speckles of gold around his irises were all that remained.

"The final falling of Wrath, the Third Original. That is what this day shall bring." Hermes confirmed.

The God roared as his eyes faded to red, his brow tensing. With a thumping kick, he sprung from his hole, reaching out to grab both of his siblings heads. His speed was insufficient, his injuries taking their toll.

The two dodged and commenced their own attacks. Lilith drove her knee into Wraths stomach, whereas Hermes slammed his fist between his brothers' eyes.

Wrath was knocked back, recovering the landing as his boots carved into the rubble. He slapped a hand over one eye, as though he were trying to sooth the pain of his brothers strike. His rage began to throb within his mind and soul, though he tried to remain focused, glancing through his fingers.

"Wrath! What's happening to you?!" Vixrol cried, slightly in the distance. His outburst grabbed the attention of the three beings. The True God and Demon showed little interest, deciding that his position as Prodigy Child was growing obsolete to their plans.

Wrath on the other hand was delivered an idea. "Commander! I need a weapon!" He was aware that his demand would hardly benefit him, though, at this stage in the battle, he could not afford to refuse assistance.

Vixrol tensed as his question was ignored, yet he obeyed his comrade. He knelt to the ground, lifting a blood coated blade.

"Not a Mortal blade! Forge me one of magic!"

The Commanders head darted up as his instructions had escalated above what he was expecting.

Hermes began to laugh. "And you truly believe that any weapon he can manifest will be more powerful than ours? Such foolishness shames me."

Baring his teeth, and tossing the battered helmet from his head, Vixrol was determined to prove his worth. He dropped both his blades and placed the balls of his hands together, his fingers wrapping onto his wrists. "When I last needed your help, you gifted me with something. Allow me to return it to you." A sliver of light cracked through the seam of his hands.

Wrath removed the hand from his face and held it to the sky, awaiting the creation of his item. In a green, flashing burst, Vixrol pushed his palms forward, firing a flaming essence towards the Third. It zoomed into his hand, expanding into a long, broad claymore, similar to the one Brekos had wielded.

The ground beneath him popped under its weight, yet naturally, Wrath had no trouble holding it.

"Using part of your soul as a physical weapon...interesting." Hermes congratulated, cupping his chin on his finger and thumb. "Lilith if you please."

As he kindly asked his sister to take the lead. She stepped forward towards her brother, placing one hand on the back of the other. As she stroked along to her fingertips, the armoured plates powdered into dust.

Wrath could not believe his luck. His nemesis was casually sauntering towards him, completely unguarded. In a deadly swing, he sliced the blade down on his sister. Although, with absolute minimal effort, she caught the blade against her bare palm.

Wrath eyes widened in impossible surprise. As sharply as his weapon formed, it began to break down, fluttering away in a red cloud. "No...what did you do?"

"I did nothing. You gifted that section of your soul as purity. If you could only see your own eyes now, you would realise that your soul, and that weapon, could never work in unity." Lilith explained. "That is one section of yourself that you will never regain."

The third dropped the hilt to the rock, which rang as it landed before vanishing in a bloody fog.

Hermes slowly floated into the air, his robes waving back and forth. "You are forever weakened brother. And you will never regain your place among the Gods."

Lilith sought revenge for the pain inflicted to her, before Hermes arrived. Noticing Wrath had totally lost the will to struggle on, she leapt above his head, spinning and pummelling his jaw with her shin. His cheek rippled as Liliths sharp attack drove him off his feet. He crashed to the ground, saving his fall with his hands and bare knee. Lilith curved up towards the clouds, posing next to Hermes. Wrath gradually fumbled to his clanking feet. As the red eyed God hunched helplessly on the ground, the two fighters hovered above.

"I don't believe this. When I heard that you had gained the approval of one God, I expected you to be an overwhelming opponent, a true power to be reckoned with. How wrong I was." Hermes lectured, disappointed that his brother, whom he had descended to kill.

Wraths arms began to shake with anger, while his knees buckled with exhaustion. Blood dripped from his bowed head, quickly creating a spreading puddle that seeped into the cracks below.

Hermes stared down at his brother, unwilling to continue the battle against such a wreck of a God. He was ashamed. "I grow tired of this. Perhaps when you

are not cowering like a dog, we will revisit this day."
He began to step away.

"A dog...?"

"Yes brother! A dog!" He cried as he turned back. "A
rodent, a lowly creature that at every turn causes me
greater interference! Nothing but an animal!"

The Thirds fists clenched as his resolve strengthened.
He came to a conclusion, one that he despised himself
for. Though other than death, it was his only option.
"You think me an animal?" He threw his head back.
"Fine! I'll fight like an animal!"

His pupils shrank, closing into the size of pinheads. His
red eyes blazed into light as he rolled his head back,
howling at the sky. He threw his arms out to his sides,
his hands tensed like claws.

The rock around his feet started to break apart, dust and
light rushing into the air like fountains. Before long
Wraths fury was on the outside for all to see. His
muscles bulged and ripped. The ground beneath him
trembled and creaked. His outward presence of power
created dazzling light displays, beautiful yet terrifying.

The pair of traitors watched closely in quiet
concentration, as the rest of the battlefield fled and
scurried to safety.

"Wrath! Stop this at once!" The Commander demanded.
His order was ignored. The God continued to bellow at
the sky, his hellish eyes wide with strain as he pushed
himself further beyond his boundaries. Suddenly his

irises slammed shut, vanishing totally from his eyes. Red flares boomed along with his blue flames.

"And just like that, he throws away his last hope of returning to Heaven." Hermes grinned.

"Such a fool, against two of us, even his Paladin would be lacking. What chance does he have as a mindless waste of a man." Lilith agreed, folding her arms as she glanced down to the flaming man, knowing that very soon he would become her ally.

The Fourths wicked smile grew as he witness his brother losing all connection to his mind. Wraths eyes began to glow, shining with a pure white light. It caught against the creases on his brow and cheeks as his scream turned even wilder. The current of ash and light thundered into a denser uplift. The three gashes on his face began to seal shut, the folds of skin clasping at one another.

Hermes twitched with uncertainty. "Something is wrong..."

"What are you saying?" She questioned.

"This should not be happening, he should have completed his alternation by now."

"What difference does it make?"

"Look at him. Does he seem like a God who is merely blind with rage?"

Lilith looked closer. "From what I see, he has finally gone Berserk."

"No. He was Berserk a moment ago. It is as though he has completely surrendered himself to Hell."

Their concern was interrupted by a booming wave as silence introduced itself. Wrath had ended his bursts of power, and his body had relaxed to a limp hang. His chin was tucked into his neck as he slumped over, still.

"Third…?" Hermes nudged, hovered down but also away, cautious of the sudden change is character. "Speak."

A deep grumbling snarl quivered from the doubled over God. Slim shards of rubble drifted up from the ground around him, calmly hovering higher. Suddenly the growl thundered into an almighty holler. Raising his head with swift focus, the light from his eyes streaked, giving birth to narrow, horizontal flares.

The couple shot back, distancing themselves from their brother. With a high pitched squeal, the flares shattered, tightening the atmosphere. Its immense pressure was enough to bring the living to their knees, while squashing the bodies that splattered the battlefield. As the force reached Hermes and Lilith, they were sent plummeting to the dirt, their legs straining to remain standing.

"What…is he?!" Hermes cried out in terrified frustration.

Groaning, Lilith strained to raise an arm towards the sky, her head still bowed by the weight. She too screamed, lifting her own pressure to equalise the distortion. As the heaviness lifted, their legs remained tense, throwing them up from the ground.

"Damn you…trying to bring a God to his knees." Hermes cursed, holding his hand out, aiming at his brother who quietly moaned as he developed two, sharp fangs. "Let us see what it takes to make you kneel."

His eyes widened as he unleashed a concentrated funnel of gravity, instantly pushing Wrath to all fours. The world around him hazed as he scraped his clawed nails across the ground.

"Bow!" Hermes demanded, deepening the burden. It seemed to be effective, pressing the Thirds chest ever closer to the ground, his knees twitching above the rubble as metal coated toes gripped at the rock.

"It is as though his consciousness has not been discarded. A Berserk God would never be pinned so easily." Lilith turned to the Fourth, her skin crawling as she noticed his pained expression. His lips were pulled back as he strained, pushing with all of his might to keep the Third from moving. The Demons spine tingled as she realised what her actions had caused. Wrath was able to bring his siblings to the ground with merely a shout, whereas Hermes was streaming as much invisible energy as possible onto his brother, just to keep him from moving.

Struggling, Wrath was able to raise his head, looking like a lion about to attack. His mouth grinned with twisted pleasure, yet his forehead was tense with pain and anger. Dipping his body, his limbs tensed, tightening like a catapult. Suddenly, he pounced, ripping through the pressure and wind. Before either of his siblings could react, he smashed his head against Liliths face, launching her away as she clasped her nose, shrieking.

She zoomed towards the Gate, spiralling into one of her Hounds. It jerked away, bowing its head as its Queen squirmed against its jaw. Wraths assault did not slow, he instantly appeared before his sister, his swelling, muscular arm in mid-swipe.

The outmatched woman desperately rolled out of the swings range. She heard the Thirds attack clash as she fell to the ground, her eyes close, relieved that she had been agile enough to dodge. Then a light, brushing sensation blew across her hand, sparking terror in her mind.

Darting upright, she was confronted with an abyss of black ash. Though Wraths attack had failed to wound its target, it did succeed in severing the head of the demonic gatekeeper. Its body powdered from the neck down, blankets of its skin folding on the breeze. As the mist began to vacuum into Hell, a pair of blazing eyes peered through, quickly revealing a bold, grand figure. A God insane.

It stared down at its primary victim, though she had greater concerns. As the Hound faded away, its leash peeled and whipped across the sky. The upper sheet of the Gate began to sink into the middle, with no guardian to pin it open. As the chain bounced across the

189

corpse covered soil, Lilith dived and looped her arm under it, leaning back as she pulled. Her armoured heels scraped into the ground, dragging up dirt and pebbles.

Wrath felt no sympathy for his sisters' dismay. His mind was centred on causing as much pain to his siblings as possible, wanting them to experience his authority.

He blistered down towards her, distorting the haze of ash surrounding him. During his approach, a bright golden flash stole his attention. It was Hermes, soaring towards him with his fist pulled back, ready to throw a devastating punch. Wrath was not willing to let his brother steal another lucky blow. He changed his direction, sharply turning to meet his brother. At once, they both drove their fists forth, smashing against each other.

By nature, Hermes had the upper hand, fuelled by his Godly abilities. However, Wrath was driven by sheer rage alone, with total disregard for his actions. As such, the Third overpowered his sibling, his strike shattering the opposing hand as it burst, tossing blood across both of the fighters.

Hermes bellowed with a painful outcry as he clutched his bloody stump, strands of fingers and palm sagging from its edges. His body slightly curled as he looked to his arm, shivering with pain and fear of his brother. He too realised what he had done. Gazing up, his eyes met the shining eyes of the Third, locked in domination.

Wrath slowly placed a foot between his brothers arms, only applying slight pressure. Hermes tried to move, yet his body ignored his wishes, terrified into paralysation. Beads of sweat dripped from his brow as blood spewed from his arm.

With casual action, Wraths leg bluntly extended, blasting the bloody God into the ground, rings of steaming air growing from his trail. Rubble was tossed into the air, spinning before slamming back down. As the dust cleared, his body regained stiff, refusing to move as he lay in a rocky bowl. Above him, Wrath floated, looking down in a controlled pose.

As the Fourth placed his remaining hand down, pushing himself up, his older brother beamed with streaking lights, flowing around his armour and the creases of his muscles. In a belt of light, he vanished, though unlike earlier, he did not leave a ribbon of aura where he travelled. As soon as he vanished, his fist clamped Hermes's head back to the ground.

Straddling his wounded sibling, with thump after thump, Wrath caved the Fourths head deeper into the dirt. Blood splattered from Wraths knuckles as he began to deliver brutal damage to the helpless victim.

"Brother!" Lilith cried, scrapping at the metal reins as she was dragged closer to Hell. "Send the anchor!"

From the depths of the shadowy realm, howled a rocketing, low pitched noise. It grew louder before it revealed itself. A large iron horn sailed into Liliths hand. She whipped the twirled antler over arm and through a link of the chain. It shackled the hinge to the rock, pinned the Gate open once again, allowing her to relax.

Meanwhile, Wrath continued to hammer into his brother, delivering one last blow as Hermes stopped twitching. He emerged from the crater, taking strong strides across the wasteland. Lilith looked on in unusual heartache that her holy comrade showed no signs of life.

"My King...take him." Her words were soon followed by an echoing whistle. Several additional chains bounced from the shadows, darting towards the furious God.

He swiped the first chain away with careless ease as he paced on. Another chain rattled towards him, which again was slapped away. As the third leash approached, his deflection was halted when his arm was suddenly wrapped with metallic binds. One of the chains he had cast aside, circled back and encased his limb. As soon as one was trapped, his concentration wandered, inviting the other iron whips to seize him. Shackle after shackle they tightened around him, as the final one latched to his neck.

He pulled and clawed at the chains, franticly trying to free himself. The sensation of being bound reminded him all too clearly of his false imprisonment, a feeling he was eager to remove. The chains seemed to gain a will of their own, slowly lifting him into the air. Once his feet were clear of the ground, they tightened, heaving him towards the mouth of the dark, evil realm.

Wrath twirled in the air, trying to reach down and brace his hands into the rock. It did not work, he was simply too high to reach. In a shock of instinct, he once again released a suffocating pressure, this time on himself, and without the cry. His fingertips skidded across the soil as the chains persisted, inching him into their world.

Suddenly, with furious effort, he smashed his fist into the ground, pinning him in place. The iron straps tugged at his limbs, sweat dripping from the tip of his nose, brought out through a combination of panic and pain.

Forcing his other arm to lift, he also jabbed it to the ground, slightly in front of the other. Punch after punch, he crawled away from the Gate, literally fighting for his survival. The further he wandered, the more difficult it became. Regardless of his fury, the imminent knowledge that he could be swept up and dragged into the Underrealm, was enough to tear his resolve apart.

"Wrath!" Bellowed the Commander, sprinting towards the struggling being, his sword clasped in both hands by the side of his head. With a swing of raw determination, Vixrol drove the blade towards a chain. As soon as contact was made, its shimmering edge oozed into molten steel, splashing to the ground in superheated beads.

The follow through knocked him off balance, stumbling and bracing himself on the chain, gripping it. It repelled his presence, throwing him several feet. The handle bounced from his grip as he landed, its broad, flat tip glowing with heat.

The braces tightened, attempting to crush the Thirds muscles and armour. He let out a roar as he felt his fist slipping from the safety of the rock. The light in his eyes dimmed as hope slipped away. His hair fell into its usual, softly spiked style. His body seemed to shrink as his muscles relaxed. All rage had drained from the God, returning him to his composed, calm self.

Vixrol sat up, pulling a short blade from his belt, preparing for his second attempt at freeing his comrade. He jumped to his feet, ignoring his inability to breathe.

Before he could make his charge, Wrath was ripped from the ground, his pressurised column ceasing to exist. He was pulled closer to the Gate, his heart breaking as he accepted defeat.

A wide booming light covered the sky, leaving those looking up in a slight daze. In flowing elegance, an inky white cloud crashed down from the Heavens, severing the iron whips during its descent. They darted back into the Gate, Wrath still gliding towards it with momentum. A second flash, this one with a blue tint, thundered down and halted behind him, stopping him from falling into Hell.

Two bands of light tucked under his arms, holding his securely in the air. The first source of light landed on the ground, an echoing clash ringing though the rock stayed intact. The shape of white straightened its crouched position, dense bright fog flowing from its head, concealing it from sight. It paused for a moment, standing, before the steam rolled downwards, clearing, revealing a handsome, bold man amongst it.

His eyes possessed a sunburst glow as he gazed over the battlefield, not focusing on any one scene. His costume was an even combination of cloth and metal, golden bands sealed around his shoulders, waist and ankles. They held long, glorious robes in place. Blonde, layered hair covered his head, barely long enough to blow in the breeze his landing had created. Thin stubble spread across his jaw and around his lips.

However, there was a particular feature about his head that displayed his rank. A circular, cloudy halo sat above his head, representing a small galaxy. His entire appearance was a vision of absolute perfection.

Wrath struggled to lift his head, straining his eyes open, totally drained of strength. His dull yellow eyes focused on the new arrival as he stood tall, his back to the Gate, and to the dangling God. He wheezed as he tried to speak. "B....Brother..."

# Chapter XIII
-
# Judgement

The battle fell quiet, the attention of every living being, focused on the new, holy arrival. Slowly, he turned to face Vixrol. He did not speak, his eyes merely examined. He seemed to lose interest in the Prodigy Child, turning further to look up at his brother.

"Tristen, bring him." The toned God commanded, raising an open hand towards him.

As the figure of light obeyed, it moving closer, creeping out of its smoky shroud. A slightly older man emerged, clasping the man in his arms. His long, dark brown hair swayed around his shoulders, a thin strip of beard spreading from his chin to the base of his lips.

"Tristen…I…" Wrath began.

"It is best for you to remain silent, brother. The First has set his mind on delivering this sentence. Do not encourage him to be harsh." Tristen whispered with a gentle yet strong voice.

The Third squinted and bowed his head, slightly baring his teeth as his eyes welled up. The last time his brother passed judgement on him, he was stripped of his powers and rights as a God. It only made sense that this time he would be tossed one realm lower.

196

Tristen eased to a halt several metres above the dirt, still holding Wrath tightly, as his superior lowered his arm. One of his arms was entirely covered in shimmering gold armour, three, layered blades of it, extruded from his elbow. It was held in place by a pleasing, collared shoulder pad. Although, his other arm was only protected at the wrist, a shining brace clamped to it.

"Third Original, I call upon you to repent for your sins, and stand trial for your disregard of the terms of your banishment. Should you be found guilty, you will be removed from this realm and imprisoned in another." The First summoned, allowing his brother undivided attention.

Wrath closed his eyes as his fears were confirmed, a tear dripping from his eyelashes.

"I claim this trial, in session." His voice echoed with his last two words. As his announcement rang, three more shudders of light, fell from the sky, positioning themselves evenly along the wayside. Fog continued to pour from them as they seemed to look on at the trial.

"Brother Wrath, are you satisfied that all those whom are required to witness your trial, are present?"

"Yes, my King..." He whispered.

"Then let us continue. First off...what in Heavens name do you think you're doing?"

"Sir...?" Wrath questioned, raising his head though still looking down to his brother.

197

"I granted you passage to the Mortal realm, and spared you from my initial desire to banish you to Hell. And here you are. You have broken the two commandments I placed upon you during your exile." His brow tightened as he felt betrayed by his lesser ranking brother. "You swore an oath of holy grant, that you would protect mankind using the permissions I allowed, and only those abilities. Though today in the witness of thousands of Mortal eyes, you surrendered to your rage and discarded your allegiance to the Higher Realm."

"Forgive me brother, if I had not allowed my emotions to warp me, all these men would be dead."

"Enough! Do you deny pushing to Berserk?"

"No."

"And do you deny pushing beyond that level to access your mirror soul?"

"No."

"And do you-"

"I deny none of your accusations!" He cried impatiently, wishing his King would swiftly pass judgement and end his misery.

The First calmly smiled in response to the Thirds cheeky outburst. "Good, that should save us some time. Now to the second charge against you. You gave me your word, that you would not go looking for your daughter. Care to explain how it is that you were granted powers by her order?"

"Lailah? Would you rather she left the Fourth to kill me? Would you rather this world fall into Hells grasp? Or perhaps this is your own guilt attacking your mind."

The First lost his patience, though he controlled it well. Wrath noticed his brow flicker with annoyance.

"You are the God of Balance. You are the one of us whose duty is to maintain balance between light and dark, by judging others accordingly. So tell me, how is it you banished a child, a being with purest of soul, from Heaven?"

"You know the perfect reason for my actions, man." His outward appearance was controlled and settled, though his impatience grew for his brothers words.

"Because you fear her? Because she is a creation that you could not foresee. Explain to me brother, why do you fear her?"

"Because her simple existence brings my Balance an inch closer to shatter!"

Wrath smiled. "If only Hermes was as loyal to his duty as you are."

"Bear in mind that although yours is the higher rank, he has authority over you now."

Wrath fell silent as he could not argue with his brothers facts.

"I shall not waste anymore of my time on your trivial life. As such, I deliver your punishment. I, Deitus, the First Original and King of those who name me their brother. I sentence you to one thousand years reform in Purgatory."

Wraths grin of hidden fear turned to confusion. "...Purgatory?"

"It is a realm I newly created for the restructuring of ones mind and soul. Sending you to Hell would cause me no triumph." The First offered out his hand, stretching out his fingers. Slim, dancing streams of light pranced from the other Gods present, including Hermes, who had finally stumbled from his unconscious slump, still with only one hand.

The streaks of light mixed and merged into a long, waving pole. At its head, grew roots of energy, short and delicate, but shining brightly. The Judge closed his fist around it, strings of sparks forming at his touch.

"Wrath, do you accept the punishment dealt against you?"

"I accept your judgement my King." Wrath said with a smile, overjoyed that his brother had created an alternative to Hell.

Deitus pointed the rooted end of his sceptre towards the joyful God, who was streaming with tears of happiness. "Then it is decided. You have one thousand years to save yourself from damnation. Do not disappoint me, brother." With his decision passed, the twisting rods of light stretched the distance between the two. They ripped into the centre of Wraths chest, yet they did not reach through to his back.

The Third stiffened, naturally wanting to dodge the incoming sabres, yet he continued to smile. As the narrow spears retracted from his torso, Tristen too released his grip. Wrath began to fall, though after a moment, his body dissolved into a waving shimmer of white glitter. It quickly spread out, thinning to the point of being invisible.

"What did you do to him!?" Snarled a soldier from the side lines.

The King of Gods turned to him, his golden eyes peering through a squint. "Prodigy Child. Why is it of concern to you?"

"He may be your brother, but he is also mine! We fight together, we die together!"

"It is not yet Wraths time of dying. Your life will not outlast his."

"That is all you see of man isn't it? You see that we are born, we die, and we are a nuisance to you while we live. You care not for our struggles, or the imbalance of our world."

"Watch your tongue, Human!" The First warned, turning his shoulder so the staff now faced his rude challenger.

"When I was a boy I used to dream of the day that the Gods would come to the aid of man, bringing their Angels and gifts to our realm. But now that you are here, you deliver nothing but war and death." Vixrol raged, pacing towards the God, a blade in his hand. "I am tired of Gods and Demons, and Angels and beasts. Why do you pollute our land with your law and judge what you do not understand!"

As Vixrol was within striking distance, Deitus was the one to make the first move. Yet again, the glowing fibres burst from his weapon, riddling the Commanders chest. He was knocked back mid-step, planting his foot back to the rock.

He felt breathless, looking down at the rods piercing him.

"Consent to deal punishment upon this man?" The God questioned to his brothers and sisters, keeping his eyes locked on the new defendant.

The shining clouds chimed with pinging allow, permitting the punishment to carry.

"Denied." Tristen groaned as he floated to the ground, his bare feet taping against it.

Deitus turned to his brother. "Explain?"

"Purgatory is not designed for the purge of Human sin. If you were to send him there, he would be no more pure than he is now."

"Purgatory will show him the true way to execute his life and ensure his passage from this realm into rebirth, he need not have his sins cleared."

"Maybe so yet if-"

"Overruled." The King decided, silencing his brother. He shifted his attention back to the stricken Human. "You shall join Wrath in Purgatory, for a sentence of one thousand years. When you emerge I expect you to change your violent ways." The staff shortened once again, tugging gently at the Commanders chest as they retreated.

Vixrol looked up, realising his fate had been decided by someone other than himself. Furious at his lack of control, he lunged his dagger towards the Gods throat. Before he could make contact, his armour, his dagger, and his body, exploded into a twinkling fog. It blew around the scene, gradually fading away.

As the second man had vanished from the world, the sceptre divided into glowing vines, returning to their respective Gods. The sections of the pole were returned, all except to Hermes, his strands remained in his brothers grasp.

"My King, why do you hold my sliver of the key?" Hermes panted, his hand tightly clamped around his crushed stump.

"You have conspired with Demons in order to complete your oath to the Human Lord. As far as our law is concerned, you have broken none. Though you have lost my trust, and as such I shall not grant you

Purgatory's key, nor shall you gain passage into my home. You are hereby removed from Heaven until further notice." Deitus finally turned to Hermes to make his decisions heard. "You may keep your powers, as well as your duty to ensure the progression of this realm."

The God King burst into a cloud of flowing energy, leaping into the sky before crashing down next to his wounded subordinate. As his white fog cleared, he reached out and grabbed the severed wrist, and pulled it from Hermes's grasp. He held it tightly beside his head.

Veins of light spread up from its opening, wrapping and forming into a fully functional hand. Hermes looked in awe as his body was repaired, his brothers eyes blazing behind the growing hand. Once it was complete, a thin coating of aura shattered away from it.

"This is the last gift I shall give to you." Deitus cast the Fourths arm aside, Hermes slightly leaning to follow the momentum. "You may call yourself a God, but you may never call me brother."

The pairs eyes locked for a moment in silent battle, though the King quickly broke off his gaze to address the thousands that stood around the landscape. "I have removed two of your greatest warriors from this world, and in doing so, removed your chances of victory!"

He turned to focus his following speech on Lilith, though it was for all to heed. "As the God of Balance, I must correct the unstable nature of this land, by ending this hellish war!" He tucked his hand up between his head and shoulder, then he harshly slapped it out again.

Wave upon wave of creature boomed into ash, their remains tumbling back into the Gate.

Liliths face stiffened and her body shuddered as her former King was able to annihilate her entire army with a single swipe of his arm. Within moments, the battlefield was cleansed of all evil matter, except for Lilith and her two remaining Hounds.

Tristen turned to face the Gate, his head slightly hanging. In a whip of his metallic arm, a magnificent golden bow spawned in his hand, sparks dashing off it as it manifested. He stretched out his arm, twisting his weapon horizontally. He wrapped three fingers under the glowing string, pulling it back as he raised his hand to eye level, aiming down his sights. A pair of glimmering arrows sparkled into creation, aiming slightly in opposite directions.

In utter silence, the twin arrows grew denser, shining brighter. In a sudden flick, Tristen released the string, firing the projectiles towards the canines. They delivered but a swift whistle as they speared through the air. As they stabbed shallowly into beasts flesh, the whistle dimmed into a low ping.

The gatekeepers seemed unfazed by the small, glowing splinters sticking from them. All of a sudden, the arrows detonated, erupting into enormous blasts of power. The Hounds were ripped apart, blooming into ash as the ground beneath them crumbled and bounced like ripples on water.

Lilith shielded her face by crossing her arms in front of herself. Though as the ground sprung, she was tossed from it, falling back into Hell. He looked back, her eyes widening as she realised that without Wrath, the anchor was her only connection to the Mortal realm. She held out her hand, reaching towards the iron horn. The shock of the blast began to peel layer after layer of armour from her.

She saw a shape appear through her fingers. Looking up, she realised it was her brother, the King of her old home. His movements were dazzled with fibres of waving light. In the background, the mysterious clouds of white, flourished back into the sky, escaping the collapsing ground.

With an almighty kick, Deitus booted the peg back into the shaded abyss. It cracked in half as it was forced through the chain, blazing red fragments shattering away from it.

The Gate creaked and groaned, squealing as it could not sustain itself any longer. It burst at the seams, folding in on itself. The edges of the crack flooded with flames that entwined as the split narrowed, being pulled shut.

Lilith looked out. Beholding a set of raging yellow eyes and a shining halo as she fell, fires blooming towards her feet as the air shifted. The tear in reality was closed by the hands of her brothers, trapping her away for yet another eternity. With no army and no road to freedom, she would lie in wait, gathering her strength before she would once again plummet the Earth into warfare. With this, she silently promised, that regardless of the time she must wait, she would bring the Doors of Heaven crashing down. She swore that one day, she would take her brothers life.

Lightning Source UK Ltd.
Milton Keynes UK
UKOW030808061012

200153UK00001B/6/P